I0575363

Edward Ledwich Mitford

Poems, Dramatic and Lyrical

Edward Ledwich Mitford

Poems, Dramatic and Lyrical

ISBN/EAN: 9783744788069

Printed in Europe, USA, Canada, Australia, Japan

Cover: Foto ©Andreas Hilbeck / pixelio.de

More available books at **www.hansebooks.com**

POEMS

DRAMATIC AND LYRICAL.

POEMS

DRAMATIC AND LYRICAL.

BY

EDWARD LEDWICH MITFORD.

LONDON:

PROVOST & CO., successors to A. W. BENNETT,
5, BISHOPSGATE WITHOUT, E.C.

1869.

LONDON :

R. BARRETT AND SONS, PRINTERS,

MARK LANE.

CONTENTS.

——◦◦◦——

" WHAT can a man do that cometh after the king? even that which hath been already done." Ideas and even words have been so used up that it is very difficult for any writer in the present day to avoid being charged with plagiarism. Shakespeare has become an integral part of the English language, and his thoughts and words will crop up like sunlit rocks on a plain, whenever it is attempted to write English in its simplicity, while echoes from the reading of our other old poets inevitably creep into our 'own compositions. In poetry, as in painting, we may remodel and compile, but we cannot improve on our old masters, and rarely originate a new idea. When I am conscious in these pages of being indebted to " the great men which were of old," I have noted the passages, and will gladly acknowledge any others that may be pointed out by my critical or indulgent readers.

E. L. M.

MITFORD, *10th June. 1869.*

PRINCE EDWARD.

Dramatis Personæ.

HENRY III.

PRINCE EDWARD, *his Son.*

SIR ADAM DE GOURDON.

SIMON DE MONTFORT, *Earl of Leicester.*

GILBERT CLARE, *Earl of Gloster.*

SIR ROGER MORTIMER.

SIR JOHN MAUNSELL, *Secretary.*

SIR AYLMER L'ESTRANGE.

SIR HUGH DE TURBERVILLE.

ROBERT LEYBURN.

HUGH BASSET.

EDRIC BASSET, *a Minstrel.*

WILFRID.

WALTER, *Head Forester.*

MARION, *his Wife.*

MARGARET BASSET.

ROWENA, *her Attendant.*

A Captain, Foresters, and Guards.

A.D. 1265.

PRINCE EDWARD.

ACT I.

Leic. Prince Edward has escap'd—abused my trust
That foolishly allowed him exercise.

Gour. How 'scap'd he ?   By treachery ?

Leic.   I know not ;
But whether treachery, or negligence,
His guards now hang for it.   They might have known
That when they gave an Englishman a horse,
They gave him means to win his liberty.

Bas. And a prince too !   A yeoman had done it.

Gour. It was not well unless his word were
    pledged ;
With him that were security enough.

Leic. O ! the folly of it annoys me most :
But peril imminent awaits such carelessness.

The mischief done, let preparation due
Find us full arm'd to remedy this breach.

   Gour. Already are we weaken'd by division :
Gloster, whom your pride has alienated,
Is now in arms against us.   United,
You held all England at command.   But now——

   Leic. The Earl of Gloster check'd at no pride of
     mine,
But at his own ambitious lure flew wide.
No cause can brook two leaders ; and if I
Had stoop'd to bear an equal in command,
Which he aspir'd to, confusion had ensued.

   Gour. My lord, your pardon ; is it not then true
That you refused the Earl some prisoners
With scant courtesy ?

   Leic.   Not so.   I refused
To cede Earl Richard, brother of the King ;
To have given up so high a prisoner
Were to have given up the leadership.

   Bas. Let him go :—'tis better to encounter
Perils with an united few, than lead
A larger force, and with divided councils.

   Gour. Yet fortune favours numbers.   The Prince
     free
Will gather followers on his road, and join
The pow'r of Gloster, now at Kenilworth.

LEIC. His name's a host.   We must forthwith away
To meet them ere their forces are increased.
I'll toward Worcester :—Follow with your men
Before the night.   And you, Sir Ralph, will summon
De Crespigny and Mandeville.   My sons,
As past their camp I go, I'll take with me.

BAS. My lord, we follow you with all despatch.

                  [Exit LEICESTER, TURBERVILLE.

GOUR. Before we go, the lady Margaret
Your cousin I would see, to take my leave.

BAS. I dread her tears.   The thought of battle
Fires my blood, but woman's tears congeal it.
Poor girl ! How I pity these poor women
That fain must sit at home, while those they love
Are in the wars ; waiting on life and death,
List'ning for halting news.   Lo where she comes.

           Enter MARGARET.

Kiss me, coz, and God be wi' ye.   I'm for the field.

                    [Exit BASSET.

GOUR. Dear Margaret, I again must leave you.

MARG. Why, my beloved, this haste ?   What has
    befallen ?

GOUR. Know you not the Prince has 'scap'd ?

MARG. Of that I was thinking.

GOUR. Ah ! you knew it : Why should it give you
    thought ?

MARG. Is it not dangerous to the Barons' cause,
The cause of freedom ?

GOUR.   Are you not sorry
That the Prince is gone ?

MARG.   No : why should I be ?
Sorry I am that he has gone to swell
The flood that threatens us.   O that this war
Were ended.   How I feel the daily peril
In which you live.

GOUR.   Margaret, your love has made me
Almost coward—the love of worth and truth
And excellence shrin'd in a beauteous form.
O separation ! cold heartbreaking word !
I feel like one fall'n from the cliffs of hope,
Sav'd from despair's dark gulf by cords of love;
Now in mid air I seem suspended hung,
And horror chills me as I see the knife
Of separation pressing its keen edge
Against the strained cords;   the strands   part   and
      unwind :
My sight grows dizzy as I upward gaze
On the last thread that yet upholds my life.
O separation ! my heart sinks : that word
Is temporary death.   Danger I feared not ;
Life was well lost, given in duty's cause :
'Twas but " an empty casket "—now 'tis fill'd

With the rich jewels of your love—and I,

Ó how I fear to lose it !

   Marg..   To wish you go

I cannot,—yet I cannot urge you stay :

And my poor bosom 'mid this civil strife

Is torn by adverse wounds.   For you to shrink

From duty were to tarnish honour's shield,

And from the bright shrine of my soul depose

Your desecrated image.—Wish you go !—

O no : I am no Spartan : nor they women.

Time's harrow swerves not from its course for tears

Or sighs or vows—Go therefore,—let no thought

Of me make weak your heart.

   Gour.   No, Margaret,

Your presence ever felt will be a light

To guide my steps.   Your love will be a power

Leading me upward to the highest scale

Of duty's ladder, making me worthy of it.

And so—while I'm myself—farewell !

   Marg. Farewell ! my best beloved.

                               [*Exeunt.*

SCENE 2.—*Winchester. The Hall of State.* KING HENRY
   III., Secretary SIR JOHN MAUNSELL, GILBERT CLARE
   EARL OF GLOSTER, PRINCE EDWARD, SIR ROGER
   MORTIMER, and Nobles. *Officers bearing the standards
   and trophies of the Earl of Leicester.*

P. EDW. (*kneels*).   My liege and father,
I come to lay my trophies at your feet;
The banners of your late revolted barons,
Who now lie low upon the field of Evesham.

  K. HEN. My noble boy, well hast thou flesh'd thy
   sword—
Thy laurell'd sword, in rebels' blood.   Treason
No longer hugg'd in Fortune's arms may dread
The avenging wrath of outrag'd majesty.

  P. EDW. Vengeance is surfeited.   A fearful field
Was that whereon we triumph'd.   Earl Simon
In the battle fell; there fell, slain, his son,
With threescore gentlemen of high estate,
And twelve knights bannerets, his followers,
With many others of inferior rank.
The realm restored to its lawful king,
Let mercy spread her mantle o'er the past.

  MAUN. While I commend his Grace's generous
   spirit,

That would forgive his fallen enemies,
The safety of the State forbids the King
Should sheathe the sword of justice.

P. EDW. The safety of the State is more secure,
Encompass'd by our people's loyalty,
Than buoy'd up by their fears.

MORT. Is all that we have borne to be forgot?
Harried have been our lands, our tenants slain :
The victory ours, shall we now forego
Revenge?

P. EDW.   Revenge! You, Roger Mortimer!
Have you not had it? Blood up to the throat!
Glutted with it! Did you not on the field,
Against all laws of knighthood—My liege,
I shame to tell it—the Earl's head strike off,
And mutilate a fallen enemy?

MORT. My liege——

P. EDW. Revenge! Did you not send that head,
Ta'en from the noblest man of these curst times,
A present to your wife? I thought the world
Could breed but one Herodias.

MORT.   My lord,   .
This presence and your place——

K. HEN.   Peace, Sir Roger ;
'Twas a base deed, unworthy of a man
Of gentle blood.

Mort.   My liege, my services
Might claim more lenient judgment.·

P. Edw.   My escape
You help'd—O 'tis a bitter thing to feel
An obligation to a murderous hand !

Maun. No debt, my lord ; 'twas but a soldier's duty.
But if his Grace these traitors must forgive,
'Twere wise at least to confiscate their goods
To the King's use, and leave them powerless.

P. Edw. Sir John, the counsels that you give the
    King
Redound not to his honour.   You were cause
That disaffection spread throughout the land
Through former confiscations.   Those who lost
Their lands, lost hope, save in rebellion.
While others joined, fearing their fate to share,
And you would raise this hydra once again
To assail the scarce saved throne.

Maun.   Nay, my lord,
The Earl's ambition raised this head of war.

P. Edw. The Earl was not ambitious. I must say it—
With due respect unto this royal presence—
In justice to a noble foe.   Leicester
Fought for the nobles' and the people's rights.
We—broke faith with them, and violated
The Charter which we swore to keep at Oxford.

K. HEN. Son, you have gain'd the victory with your
   sword;
Finish the work so valiantly begun.
We leave the recusants to your disposal.
As for the oath we swore to them at Oxford,
We hold ourself no longer bound by it,
Being therefrom absolved by the Pope.

   P. EDW. O good my liege, let priestcraft dwell with
   monks:
Man cannot change that which is wrong to right:
There is a law above all popes t' annul,
The law of God and conscience. If the Pope
With impious pow'r absolve us from an oath,
And sanctify a lie, can we complain,
When, for his selfish ends, he shall absolve
Our subjects from the oath they've sworn to us?
Hereafter who will trust a prince's word?

   MAUN. My lord, his Majesty was forc'd to swear
While under durance: though upon that plea
He might refuse to ratify his act;
His conscience, ever tender of offence,
The case submitted to his Holiness.

   P. EDW. Thus we have seen the Emperor Conrad's
   subjects,
Who took their oath of compell'd fealty,
Reliev'd from it by this audacious priest,

And all his states in civil warfare plung'd :
The Empire under ban.

MAUN.   And can a King
Leave this dire weapon in the people's hands,
And fail to use it in the State's defence ?
My lord, 'twere foolish policy, methinks.

P. EDW. A King cannot so juggle with his faith.
For me, at least, I hold myself full bound.
Had I given my word, as knight and noble,
'Twere sacred : I have sworn—and keep my oath.

K. HEN. I look back on the time, my son, when I
Was such an one as you : long years, since then,
Have taught me see things with a clearer view.
Believing in their truth, did I, unwise,
A compact make with these rebellious lords.
Have we had peace since then ?   Or was it not
A mean to get all power into their hands,
And make their King a puppet?   These barons
Broke their own compact on the field of Lewes,
Where fell five thousand of my English subjects.
They broke their compact when with traitorous hands
They made ourself a prisoner.   Our oath
They have washed out in blood, and forfeited
Their own engagements.   Nathless we will keep
Such articles as may be for the weal
Of all our people.

Gloster, you have redeem'd

By this day's services your late rebellion

On that bloody field. I would wish to think

That your allegiance to our crown were based

On higher motives than your enmity

To the fall'n Earl, your former friend and chief.

Mortimer! with barbarous hand you've stain'd

This fair, but dear-bought victory. Instead of fame

Ennobling your posterity, shall deathless shame

Track you throughout all time on history's page,

Until you meet your noble foe before

The Throne of Him to Whom all must account.

Meantime, till penance done, dishonour not

Our Court or presence.   *[Exit* MORTIMER.

Edward, you have won what men call glory.

Woe worth the day ! when Glory's sacred name,

The attribute of God, was misapplied,

Compell'd to grace the slayer's ruthless sword,

And made the badge of blood ! All praise to Him !

Your valiant arm has once more sav'd our crown.

In the Cathedral shall these banners hang

In memory of our deliverance.   *[Exeunt.*

SCENE 3.—*A Room in Hereford Castle.* MARGARET, ROWENA,
EDRIC *the Minstrel.*

MARG. O this suspense is terrible to bear.
To man 'tis given by action to blot out
The sense of apprehension ; on our hearts
It weighs with its full force.   Alas for me,
That like the rock-bound maiden, I must wait
The monster rumour with her barbed tongue,
To tear my heart with tidings of the fall
Of all I love.

    Row.   Dear lady, think not thus ;
Nurse not these fears.   Has not the Earl returned
Ever victorious ? Why should he now
Be conquer'd ?

    MARG.   I have a speaking terror
On my soul, that will not let me hope.   Then
They were united, and he led the pow'r
Of England's baronage.   Now, his right hand,
Gloster,—dropp'd off like to a leprous limb
Gangren'd by pride—has join'd his enemies.
Alas !

—— Does your father's harp, my Edric,
Retain its charm in your less practis'd hand ?

EDRIC. Not yet, dear lady, can I hope to soar
So high a flight as did that dear old man,
Who, as he neared heaven's gate, had caught the
    strains
Of angels, and the light that glorified
His silver hairs.

MARG. Light songs are fittest for a sadden'd heart:
The sober muse delights the light and gay.

EDRIC. O how I wish that my unskilful lay
Might soothe your sadness. List a song of mine.

MARG. Has it a name?

EDRIC.   'Tis of a Flower and Brook (*Sings*).

    I would you were a fair Forget-me-Not,
        With azure eyes,
    And I the bright Brook at your bathing feet
        That happy lies.

    Then as I warbled by, from hour to hour,
        With music sweet;
    I'd sing my love-tale to your gentle heart,
        And kiss your feet.

    And when my bosom swell'd with tearful showers,
        With tears of bliss,
    You'd bend your graceful head in timid guise
        To meet my kiss.

    Until the Brook became a torrent strong
        By summer storm,
    Embracing as it joyous swept along
        Your yielding form;

O then, soft sinking in my crystal wave,
    Within my breast
Your life enshrin'd with mine should be for aye :
    And happy rest !

MARG. A sweet air, and a love for all weathers ;
The conceit is prettily follow'd out ;
Is this your ideal of love ?

    EDRIC. It is, lady : is it not true ?

    MARG. Rarely, I fear.

    EDRIC. My heart spoke it ; can that mislead ?

    MARG.   It may ;
How old are you, my pretty minstrel ?
Why do you blush ? Has love already
Darken'd this young heart ?

    EDRIC.   Rather illum'd it,
As with a light from heav'n.

    MARG.   Whom love you ?

    EDRIC. You make me laugh. Whom could I love
    but you ?

    MARG. You jest, my Edric ; you are yet a boy.

    EDRIC. I am sixteen, and would it not be strange
If that I loved you not ? 'Twould seem to me
As strange, as not to love my God.

    MARG. But you must learn not to love me, Edric.
You know that to Sir Adam I'm betroth'd ;
He alone may love me.

EDRIC.   I see not that ;

Is't a reason, because that you love God,

I may not love Him too ? I must love you.

Row. Foolish boy ! What do you know of love ?

EDRIC. What do I know of love ? Love is the soul

Of music, and the music of the soul.   (*Sings.*)

> Love is the spirit of all song,
>   Bursting forth
> From all hearts upon the earth that throng,
>   From South to North.
> Love is the guiding star that leads man on
>   To stand or fall ;
> In every high and noble cause
>   Enduring all.   (*He stops suddenly.*)

What do I hear ?   What horror blasts my sight ?

Woe, woe ! the battle-field ! they fall—they fall !

(*He strikes the harp to a wild, mournful air, and sings.*)

Die, Hero, die ! Who would not die like thee ?

Mourn, England, mourn ! Who will not mourn for thee ?
        Star of humanity.

Flow, rivers, flow ; murmuring mournfully :

Thy hero slain, fighting for liberty
        Weep in thy misery.

Shame, bitter shame, on who betrayed thee ;

Branded their names shall be with infamy,
        Then lost to memory.

While from thy tomb a halo of mystery

Wraps in its blaze thy country's history :
        True son of chivalry.

Die, Hero, die ! The world is not worthy thee.

Men that live not, hereafter shall rev'rence thee
        Martyr of liberty.

C

MARG. What rapture has seized on my wild cousin
To fright me with this melancholy dirge!

EDRIC. A flash—a dream! 'tis past. (*Aside*) I fear,
    I fear
When fire burns the heart, the cause is near.
O that we could my vision realise,
And civil war throughout dear England cease.
Yes, it shall be. I see the distant time
When all these castles that now stud the land,
Threat'ning destruction from their stony brows,
Shall be cast down in ruin beautiful.
Each tower and arch, mantling in ivy soft,
Nestling in trees, or crowning swelling mound,
Shall smile o'er peaceful hamlets, and give themes
To after poets, in their lays, to sing
The warlike story of the present times.
Lo! it comes! The dream was true.

Enter Messenger.

MARG. What is't? Your face speaks swifter than
    your tongue;
And yet I dread to hear its confirmation;
Oh! could you not put on a placid mask,
And not embody horror? All is lost:—
Speak:—is he?—Who is dead? Quick—your news?

MESSEN. Pardon me, lady, that my tongue must tell

These evil tidings.   The battle is lost ;
The Earl is slain, with many more of note :
Sir Adam lives, a prisoner to the Prince,
With others now in bonds at Kenilworth.

EDRIO. O when shall England see his like again
For true nobility !—I can but weep.

MARG. (*who has stood in dumb anguish*). I cannot weep.
Leicester—dead ?   Adam—a prisoner ?—
His life—in danger ?—Edric, my horse ! quick !
I must do something.—Haste ! as you love me :—
Haste—no time to lose—Bring two mounted grooms,
And come with me. —Away.   [*Exeunt.*

——o——

SCENE 4.—*Winchester.   A room in the Castle.*   PRINCE
EDWARD, SIR JOHN MAUNSELL.

P. EDW. I must be mad ! Strike me ; that I may feel
The sting of insult, to awake my soul
From this strange lethargy.   The Earl—Leicester—
Had he but known—could easily have bound
My dastard spirits without chains or guard.

MAUN. My lord, what mean you ?

P. EDW.   Thrall'd ! What do I mean ?—
You know I was a prisoner to the Earl,
In Hereford Castle, but you know not

That Castle was a heav'n—from the which
I, like the fall'n angel, made escape,
Damn'd by ambition !

    MAUN.   I understand not.

    P. EDW. O Margaret, Margaret ! Wherefore did I quit
The empyrean where you liv'd and breath'd,
Transmuting even slavery's chains to gold,
To fall again to level of this earth ?

    MAUN. A woman ;—I begin to apprehend :—

    P. EDW. You ! you cannot apprehend : you must have
My eyes, my faculties, my soul,—to feel
All that I felt when first the cloud of light,
That shrin'd her beauteous form, envelop'd me.

    MAUN. Nor do I wish it. I would rather keep my wits
Unclouded : thus I may be more able
To help you to obtain your end.

    P. EDW.   Help me ?—
You help me ?—How ?

    MAUN. Leicester, my lord, is dead :
His ward is unprotected.   'Twere easy
To procure her company.

    P. EDW.   Procure ?—
O damned pander !—earth-born, earth-soul'd !
Procure !   Procure the sun from heav'n !
You can tamper with the devil for his aid ;

He cannot help you to command a thing
So high, so holy, as this maiden's love.

MAUN. My lord, your passion speaks. I've not deserv'd
These terms. I thought to serve you,—judging
By worldly rules which govern men. Excuse
My misapprehension.

P. EDW.   Yes, common men,
Who judge of heav'n by the rule of hell,
Or earth, which is no better. I tell thee
That but for women in this world, mankind
Were devils. Woman alone on earth
Ethereal in beauty walks—an .angel
Visible—hallowing all creation.

MAUN. As you will, my lord. Yet have I heard
　　　it said
That all the mischief done in our poor world,
Is caus'd by priests or women. I, my lord,
Am married.

P. EDW.   Yes. I grant your shavelings
For their own selfish ends embroil the world ;
But woman no more causes strife on earth
Than does religion : though men fight for both,
And desecrate the highest.

MAUN. My lord, I'm married, and I know full well
All that your angels hide—under their wings.

P. Edw. They hide the wounds man's cruelty inflicts.

Maun. Daggers they hide, and well know how to
    use them ;

Daggers whose keenest edge is whetted on

Their image, stamped on man's marble heart.

Our love gives them the pow'r they so abuse.

Good my lord, experience must be bought :

The glorious halo that surrounds the moon

Exists but in the clouds that veil her face,

And vanishes as these float on to space.

P. Edw. And then she stands more beautiful, reveal'd

In her own pure, her self-effulgent light.

I thank you for this image—to confute

Your wordly wisdom.

Maun. Let me finish it.

Hard and cold she stands—a matron brazen-fac'd !

P. Edw. Methinks, Sir John, you have not drawn a
    prize.

Maun. No, faith, because there is no prize to draw.

Woman is but as gravel in the wheels

Of a man's microcosm.

P. Edw.   Slanderer,

Your prize is wealth ; you cannot draw them both ;

That were against all laws proverbial.

Maun. Buy your experience. You check'd me late

For tendering you my aid—suspecting me

Of evil in intent ; perhaps not meant.

What hinders now, that you should marry her

If no disparagement ?   Learn for yourself

The difference between the maid and wife.

The panther sleeping on its velvet paws,

And tiger strip'd, roaming the wilds for prey,

Are not more different: for every smile

The gentle maiden lavishes, the wife

Will match with frowns.   The maiden's tongue drops
    honey ;

Gall the wife's.

   P. Edw. Hold ! let me buy experience

At whatever price, rather than take yours

For nothing.   I have more faith in woman.

   Maun. Faith ?   Even her beauty is damnable.

Has no one but yourself eyes, and a tongue ?

Eyes to see beauty, and a tongue to win it,

While vanity and self-love lurk within

Quite ready to surrender up their trust ?

The lady, no doubt, is honest.   Marry her ;

And then your children—or, I should say, hers.—

Wise men those Indians ! whose inheritance

And pedigree follow the female line ;

For truly every child its mother knows ;

But there's no certainty in male descent.

My lord, it would be treason should I doubt

The honour of my future queen.   Not so ;

I speak but of the world at large, my lord.   [*Exit.*

  P. Edw. He has a little cool'd me.   Strange it is

How women seem to change their character

When wed.   Why, 'tis apparent to the eye ;

The modest downward look, and gentle voice,

Die with the blossoms of the bridal wreath ;

And in their stead, the bold eye unabash'd

And tenor-tonèd tongue usurp their place.

Then comes suspicion, with as many ears

As Argus eyes, whispering, you have known

Ladies as fair and bright as Margaret,

Wearing the outward mask of innocence,

Whose fame a word from your seal'd lips would blast.

And why should I expect a better fate ?

Just as each thinks that all mankind must die,

While he alone's immortal ; so each one,

Though all men's wives should be unfaithful found,

Believes his own to be immaculate.

                Enter an Attendant.

  Att. The Lady Margaret Basset waits without.

  P. Edw. Who ?   Conduct her hither.   (*Exit
    attendant.*)   What may she want ?

Fool! this long hop'd-for opportunity

Cometh unask'd, and finds me 'reft of speech.

Enter MARGARET.

MARG. My lord, I come a suitor to your grace.

P. EDW. To me?

MARG. (*aside*)   He looks anger'd, agitated.

Have I in aught offended?   May I speak?

P. EDW. (*aside*) To me?   So we change parts.   My

cue is gone.

Lady, command!   I know not the great boon

Within my pow'r to grant that is not yours.

MARG. Prince, I arrest your word with fore-paid

thanks;

I ask the freedom of a prisoner

In the late battle taken.

P. EDW. (*aside*)   Perhaps her cousin.

Lady, his name?

MARG.   Sir Adam de Gourdon.

P. EDW. Ha! Why for him? Is he your kinsman?

MARG.   No.

My lord, he is——

P. EDW. (*aside*) She hesitates,—blushes:

A dire suspicion creeps into my mind.

Lady, no more—(*aside*) or I shall break my word—

Until my promise I've redeem'd.   No more.

> (*The Prince writes out the order of*
> *release and gives it to her.*)

Now is my honour safe.

MARG.   Prince, I thank you ;
But how may I repay this gift ?   My prayers, —
The grateful feelings of a maiden's heart,
Be ever yours for this so generous act.

P. EDW. You might repay me ; but——

MARG. O, tell me how !

P. EDW. (*aside*) I fear to approach the truth of what
    I dread.

Lady, you say this knight, whose liberty
You came to win, is not your kinsman :
Would it be discourtesy in me to ask
The motive of your intercession,
Gracing its object by your gentle care?

MARG. My lord, I may deny you nothing.

P. EDW. Not being your father—cousin ? a friend,
    perhaps ?

MARG. More.   Excuse my maidenly confusion ;
He is my betroth'd.

P. EDW. (*aside*)   Torment ! her betroth'd !
No circumlocution : as one that stabs
A corpse she deals this deadly blow ; cold, straight

To the heart's quick, and knows not that she wounds—
How deeply wounds!

 Marg.   What ails my lord? You're ill.

 P. Edw. No—yes—ill. Do not go; 'twill pass
  anon.

 Marg. Can I no help?——

 P. Edw.   O, yes; you can help—stay,
I am better now. How said you—betroth'd?

 Marg. Yes, Prince.

 P. Edw.   But not married. Many are
  betroth'd,
And never married.

 Marg.   O, but we shall be.

 P. Edw.   Do you love him?

 Marg. Pardon, my liege; you have upon me laid
An obligation I can ill repay;
And yet methinks it were more generous
Not to offend a maiden's modesty,
Pressing your claims within the sanctuary,
Where scarce would tread a mother's foot unshod.

 P. Edw. Forgive my sacrilege. It needs no more:
(aside) And he was in my power! Well, no matter;
I wish it not undone. O, Margaret!
Did you but know the anguish you have pour'd
Into this wretched heart; a hard return

For the late boon I gave;—you'd pity me.

But you—in your innocence—have little dream'd

How much, how long, how deeply I have lov'd you.

    MARG. You, Prince !—(*aside*) Now Heaven protect

      me !

    P. EDW.   I, your Prince,

That now abase me lowly at your feet,

Begging the mercy for myself that late

I granted to your prayer.   Hear me, Margaret.

    MARG. I dare not hear you speak to me of love.

    P. EDW. Not speak of love !   O if I cease to speak

      of love,

I must be ever dumb: for all my thoughts

Are love.   I have no feeling, sense or being,

That is not rich in love ; and all its gems

Pour'd at your feet.   O dearest Margaret,

Let not your gentle heart teach your sweet eyes

To treat my love with scorn.

    MARG. Forbear, my lord.   I have no ambition

To place myself upon your giddy height,

A mark for envy, and the victim of

A late repentance.

    P. EDW. O could you with mine eyes

But see yourself, you would not thus blaspheme

Your radiant beauty with dark suspicion

Of my disloyalty.   O could *you* so stoop,
I'd barter my reversion of the crown
To be a franklin, with your love all mine.

MARG.   I have already said my hand is pledg'd.

P. EDW.   A contract between parents: this binds not.
Or if it did, I have the power to break the bond,
And will absolve them.   Love alone can bind.
Spare me !   How long I've liv'd upon your looks,
Feeding the young hopes, nestling in my breast,
With my heart's blood——

MARG.   You speak truth.
'Tis love alone can bind—and I—forgive :
For *my* love is no longer mine to grant.

P. EDW. Ha! am I spurn'd?   It is your   Prince
    who sues,
Who may command.   Beware——

MARG.   How !—stay—my lord,
You are too noble to accept a hand
From one whose heart is given to another:
I should be more than woman, could I see
Unmov'd your suffering, and not feel for you.
Pity you ask not : more I cannot give :
Better to bear this pang with fortitude
Than sacrifice a life-long happiness
In hopeless love—for one who cannot now,
And never can return it.   Yet this more—

Be this my gratitude for your late boon
To save you from yourself.   By your good leave.

[Exit MARGARET.

P. EDW. O Margaret, dearest Margaret, stay!—
She's gone!

O that I were not human; that I were
A demon or a god, to have no sense
Of human anguish—and remorseless, slay!
O, for the fell spirit of the blind pestilence
That desolates the teeming multitude,
And in the general wreck, the loss recks not
Of one!   Or water torrent's furious force,
To plunge her down the breathless cataract;
Then gently bear her floating on the pool
'Mid curling lips of waves that laugh around;
And kiss her cold dead cheek with colder kiss,
But feel not!   O to be the tongued fire
That leaps, all scathing on its murd'rous course
With flaming joy!   Or mighty avalanche
That wraps its cold shroud round its victim's life;
Then rushes downward in a diamond blaze
Of ice-foam, with ten thousand rainbow hues
Emblazoned in the sun, and to the vale
Sinks calm—a snowy sepulchre.   To be
Any senseless thing—that kills, and smiles in killing!

[Exit.

SCENE 5.—*The Prison.* ADAM DE GOURDON.

Enter MARGARET.

MARG. Joy, joy! Adam, you're free. The gate unbarr'd:
Haste! leave this place. I cannot think you safe,
Until we breathe the blessed air of heav'n
Under the blue vault.

GOUR.   Darling Margaret,
How sweet to owe my liberty to you.
Yet stay,—tell me—say, how did you obtain
My freedom?

MARG.   No matter how. Come away:
When freedom woos, who will refuse her kiss?

GOUR. Kiss! Tell me, Margaret, to whom I owe
This——

MARG.   To me!

GOUR.   Yes; and you—to whom?

MARG. The Prince.

GOUR.   Ah!

MARG.   I will tell you: when I heard
The Earl had fallen; you a prisoner;
All my grief for my dear guardian's death
Was lost in fears for you. The Prince I knew
To be of noble nature, brave and merciful;
And to me ever kind and courteous.

Gour. Yes——

Marg.   You are not pleased.

Gour.   Pleased ? yes ; O yes—go on.

Marg. And so, with slight attendance, I took horse,
And rode from Hereford to Winchester.
My cousin Edric Basset rode with me,
With several well-armed serving-men.

Gour.   How kind
To brave these perils for my sake ! and then——

Marg. I saw the Prince ; and he, before I fram'd
My prayer to words, had granted it.

Gour.   To you?

Marg. Yes, before he knew your name.

Gour.   This is well ;
This leaves me free to act.   (*aside*) Not for myself,
Did he my freedom grant, 'twas for her sake.
The price ?   What said he to you, Margaret ?

Marg. That I will not tell you.

Gour.   Not tell me ? Why?

Marg. You have no right to ask.

Gour.   I thought I had ;
I deem'd my royalty of love—some claim
Gave me to know your thoughts, if loyal.

Marg. Doubt you my love ?

Gour.   I doubt I've cast my own
Into a gulf, where it will drag me down.

MARG. What—are you jealous?

GOUR.   Ay, most jealous :—
Like to a jewel merchant among thieves,
Whose diamonds' sparkle to their greedy eyes
May tempt their lawless hands to rob his wealth.
A full love like mine, as ocean boundless,
Rivers of love can never fill its vast,
Or make it overflow; a glorious sea
Which cannot brook to feel the smallest rill
Run backward to its source.   It gave them all
In cloud, and rain, and dew; and in return
Asks all.

MARG. You—or the sea?   You take too high a
flight.

GOUR. I do—but do not jest.   My love's a sea.

MARG. Yes; you exact too much : it is not safe
To strain a silken cord, which parted once,
Can never be re-knit.   Love is no sea,
Nor e'en a seven-fold cord, but a frail flower
Demanding gentle nurture—or it fades ;
Or grasped roughly sheds its blushing leaves
In the rash hand that marr'd its loveliness.

GOUR. I had believed in the power of love ;
And would you now persuade me it is weak?

MARG. Mistake me not.   No, 'tis not for woman
To lower the strength of that which is her life.

D

Love is all-powerful against assaults
From outward foes : hearts banded by true love
Are like the welded iron; pressure and blows
May wound and bind, but cannot separate
The linked bar; until the rust within,
Eating unseen, effects a severance.
Believe me, love is very weak indeed
'Gainst inward enemies.   Slight and neglect,
Unkindness, or reproach, or jealousy
Implying doubt; these are the rust that eat
The strongest trust away, leaving each heart
Weak and dissevered from its true support,
A helpless prey to each designing hand.

   Gour. Can I help my fears?   We have examples,
No human love is perfect : how many——

   Marg. No, never did a loving woman swerve
From bias outward, temptings, or assault,
Unless the inward traitor had betrayed
His trust.

   Gour. These are fancies.   Bear with me, Margaret,
If I myself depreciate.   The young Prince
Is handsome, of noble bearing, valiant,
And formed to sway a maiden's fantasy;
While I am rough, unpolished; and my face
No longer bears the peachy flush of youth.
Am I then wrong to fear so strong a rival?

MARG. While you would aim at modesty, your shaft
Strikes otherwise.   You are unkind.   Is this—
Is this your gratitude?   Have I deserv'd
These doubts?   And how? was I not free to choose?
Then, when approval of your rival love
Hung in suspense, your fears might have been just;
But now—when—I cannot give to words
My maiden thoughts: you are unjust—unkind—
And force tears from my eyes.

GOUR. O pardon me, my own, my only love,
That I should bring one tear to those dear eyes.
O no, it is no doubt of your true faith,
But sense of my demerits makes me fear.
It seems too high and heavenly for me—me
So unworthy—to possess your love.   When all
Young, gifted, noble—all have fail'd—is't strange
That I should ask—yes—double assurance
With the prize so high?   O does it not prove
How much I value it?

MARG. Well, well : now will I hide nothing from
  you.
The Prince asked me who you were : I told him.
Then he asked me why I sought your freedom .
I told him we were troth-plight.   He started—
Seem'd much mov'd.   And then——

GOUR.   What then?

MARG.   And then—then—
He told me that he lov'd me.

GOUR.   (*Aside*) Ah! 'tis true!

MARG. Now you start—yes—he told me of his love,
Pleading with most persuasive eloquence
That I would give him hope.

GOUR. And did you so?

MARG. How can you ask?   Again you'll anger me.

GOUR. And he has dared to speak to you of love!

MARG. And pray, sir, may none love me but yourself?

GOUR. But let them keep it deep within their hearts,
And die of it: he has dared avow it:
I owe him nothing: and I will meet him
On the battle-field, and under my sword
I'll make him swear—he'll be foresworn—
No matter—that he never lov'd you.

MARG. Is this the use to make of liberty?
Again our soil to stain with kindred blood?
And for my sake?   It is not generous;
Nor do I wish to be a swordsman's prize.

GOUR. No, Margaret.   I would not raise new war;
Nor shock your gentle nature with the thought
That blood was shed for you.

MARG. Then sheathe the sword.
The great league shatter'd, can a single head
Bear up against the power of the King?

Gour. I cannot.   No, I am in honour bound ;

The Commons I cannot forsake, and leave

My followers to the mercy of the King ;

Such mercy as the falcon shows the dove.

The realm is plunder'd, and the King forestalls

The treasures of the nobles ; of the poor

The hard-won earnings : or if aught he leaves

'Tis seized on by the harpies of the Pope.

The laity the King plunders ; the Legate

Robs the churches ; Bishops, Priests, and Abbots

Squeez'd to the quick.   The vassals at the gates

Of castles, and of monasteries—die,

And strew the highroads with " unhousell'd " dead.

Those without money cannot buy them corn ;

No corn can those with money find to buy ;

And famine hollow-eyed drives through the land

Lashing her gaunt wolves, while her lightsome car

In silence moves through mould of new-made graves.

Marg. 'Tis very sad.

Gour.   And true : shall I alone

Lie lapp'd in silken safety with my shame,

And hear De Gourdon branded with dishonour,

As recreant, betrayer of his friends ?

Marg. What shall I say ?   Come, let us leave this
   prison.

Gour. I had forgotten that it was a prison

While you were by.   Thus ever does the soul
Make its own joy or woe, apart from all
External things.

    MARG.   Am I not external,
Though animate?   How doubtful is your praise.

    GOUR. You !—soul of my soul—my being's life.
    O no !

                                 [*Exeunt.*

ACT II.

SCENE 1.—*The Park.*   AYLMAR L'ESTRANGE.

    AYLM. How lovely are thy solitudes, O England !
O my country !   Lying among the fern,
Under this elm, that whispers in the breeze,
A sunny scene I see around me spread :
On either side the trees wide-branching stand
As they have stood for centuries ; while man
Has lived his little life, and passed away.
From the hill crest, in softest verdure clothed,
The hanging copse, studded with spreading trees,
Cloth'd in their autumn brown, slopes to the stream.
And hark !—the thrilling sound—the pheasant's whirr,

Sprung from the nutty wood, and shaking down

From the bright oaks a rain of golden leaves;

While, look!—the red fox baffled steals away.

And there, a bridge, which seems as it had grown

Out of the earth in ancient times, to span

The speaking brook, that singeth underneath,

Marbled with crystal pure and emerald;

Its rushing eddies struggling with the leaves

Of waving cresses, winding with its flow,

That dip and sink and rear their garland heads

In joy, then plunge beneath the laughing stream

With lifelike restlessness; that scarce can find

The flashing dragon-fly a quiet leaf,

Whereon to rest and sun his gauzy wings.

Warbling among the pebbles, onward flows

Water and weeds commingled, the sweet brook

Kissing with truant love the bathing feet

Of fairy flowers, whose petals' painted dyes

Smile in the chequer'd sheen; and from the marge

Towers the foxglove crown'd with crimson bells;

While silken wild oats curve their spiry heads,

And fall in tassell'd showers.   But some one comes!

I hear a footfall 'mong the withered leaves.

Enter PRINCE EDWARD.

Ah, my Prince, welcome!

P. Edw.   O my dear Aylmar,
While you lie here and dream away the hours,
I'm worried with all cares.   I thought to sheathe
The sword, that sever'd late the barons' league :
But like to sparks of fire, the scatter'd chiefs
Are rising here and there, rekindling war.
My father's avarice (God pardon him !)
Encouraged by that jackal knave, Maunsel
His Secretary, by disheriting
Those who escape the field, enforces them
To turn in self-defence and spoil the realm.

   Aylm. An ill adviser is Sir John, I fear ;
And to amass more wealth he raises up
Foes to the state, and wrongs the King's good name.

   P. Edw. The nobles and the clergy are oppress'd,
And they the people plunder in their turn ;
To desperation are the Commons driven ;
And every man that offers them redress
Or bread, they'll follow to the death.

   Aylm. Who are the leaders that now rise in arms ?

   P. Edw. Leaders ! Nay, some have none.   After
       the King
Had Kenilworth invested, where held out
Simon de Montfort, Leicester's son, the Legate
Obtained terms for him, and he is banish'd :
But now the news has come—a rebel band

Has, without leader, in the fens of Ely

Taken refuge.   Another stronger force

In Hampshire, in the New Forest, harbours,

Under a man I rather would call friend ;

A stronger man lives not in England—No !

Nor a braver—Sir Adam de Gourdon.

    AYLM. I've heard of him.   He drove the Welshmen

      back

When led by William Berkeley, in their ships,

To plunder Somerset.   With a small troop

From Dunster Castle he fell upon their host,

And chased them, scattered, to their pirate barks.

Many were slain, some drown'd, the rest escaped.

    P. EDW. The same.   Oh, I'm enrag'd.   Will you

      believe it ?

He was my prisoner—and now he's free.

    AYLM. How so ?   Has he escaped, or broken faith ?

    P. EDW. Neither : my own act.   You are one, dear

      friend,

To whom I tell my weakness without shame,

For you can feel with me.   You are not like

These harden'd worldlings, whose smoke-dried reason

Brings all our actions to the square and plummet.

I told you of my love for Margaret :

I can scarce bear to speak of her—but must.

After the battle, when my heart was gay,

She came a suitor to me.   What did I?
Madly I promis'd whatsoe'er she asked
Before she told me aught.   What did she beg?
This Adam Gourdon's pardon—a prisoner
I had not seen, and thought of no account.
My word being pledg'd, I gave him freedom.
Now he has rais'd a band, a thousand strong,
Of lances, crossbow-men, and cavalry.

    AYLM. Is any sent against him?

    P. EDW.   None as yet:
But so highly vaunted is his prowess,
That I long myself in arms to meet him,
And try my skill against his giant strength.

    AYLM. Why risk a life on which so much depends
In such a petty quarrel?

    P. EDW.   Ask me why?
For the mere joy of it, enhanced by danger.
My heart bounds at the thought of meeting him,
As at the trumpet in the corded lists
At knightly tournament, sounding the charge.

    AYLM. No other motive?   Why did Margaret
Obtain from you his pardon?

    P. EDW.   She loves him.
Yes, she loves him; and dared to tell me so,
Spurning my proffered suit.   Even for this—
For this I'll meet him; love and revenge

Thron'd on my crest, urging my biting steel
To strike him dead, and pierce, through him, her heart.

AYLM. And would you on a woman be revenged?
This is not like you.   Are you not a prince?

P. EDW. Ay, but I am a man:

AYLM.   A nobler being!
King and Prince are but the names—the vestments
That man wears; the pedestal he stands on—
From whence his glory more resplendent shines,
Or darker glows his shame.   It becomes not man
To strike a woman's weak, defenceless form;
Yet you—you aim to pierce her very spirit,
Unarm'd, accessible to every wound,
And shame your manhood's high nobility.

P. EDW.   Dear friend, I well deserve your sharp
reproach.

AYLM. Forgive me, Prince; 'twas not your reason
spoke,
But wounded feeling.   Do I not know you?
Your generous spirit ready to forgive
Your vanquish'd enemies?

P. EDW.   Still your love speaks;
Yet I will meet him as my country's foe.
Should I return victorious, I will come
To you to teach me use my victory.

AYLM. I will go with you.

P. EDW.   Dear Aylmar, you're unfit
For this rough work.   Stay and immortalize
My deeds of arms, enambered in your verse ;
Or tell the nations how Prince Edward fell,
Should such his fate be.

AYLM.   We fall together.
How may I describe your valiant deeds,
Not seeing them ?   I go with you, dear friend.
Refuse me not.   Hist ! what was that that mov'd ?
See ! there—above the gorse between the trees,
A hart of ten ! restless his horns pass on,
Emerging now upon that open glade :
A glorious creature !—his head thrown back at gaze ;
With motion like a measure musical
He walks before the cowering herd—alarmed,
But following blindly their courageous head.

P. EDW. Just as these baser rebels do their chief.
But a good bow now, and a sheaf of arrows,
Were worth a dukedom.

AYLM. Let pass for once ; nor spoil so fair a picture.
Whence comes this love of ruin for disport,
That seems inborn in every English breast ?
The little child, with fiend-like innocence,
Unwings the fly ; at its vain struggles smiles ;
Or casts it in the spider's ambush'd snare,
And sees it rushed on with a breathless joy.

Then the bold boy climbing the treacherous trees,
Harries the nest, and grasps the fragile spoil ;
Or hunts the singing bird, the butterfly—
No matter what—to kill, or mar their beauty.
Next, the youth, and e'en the gentle maiden,
With bounding pulse, bright eye, and fearless foot,
Follows the swift, bloodthirsty falcon's swoop,
Or sees the merlin's talons close around
The fluttering ring-dove's throat, or pierce its heart—
With exultation.   Last comes manhood's sport,
Fierce as a passion.   The thought of boar, or wolf,
Or stag at bay, fires the eager soul
With ecstasy.   The noble horse we love
Hurl'd madly over stream, and tree, and rock ;
His life—our lives stak'd—against what ?   A prize,
When gain'd, cast out as worthless to the hounds.
And not content with creatures of our land,
We roam the Scythian wilds for beasts of chase,
The fire-eyed oryx, and the fur-clad bear,
The spotted panther, and the royal beast,
Whose spoil your grandfather, King Richard, wore ;
All for an earthly instinct that enslaves
Our finer faculties.   And to what end ?

    P. Enw. To the nurturing of gracious qualities,
Which harden man for the stern fight of life—
Courage, sagacity, and skill—towards

No sordid aim.   And then the beasts we kill
Are good for food, or noxious to mankind.

   Aylm. I grant all this ; and yet the passion rules,
Absorbing heart and mind, and which I deem
To be a remnant of that barbarous state
When every man must hunt for daily food.

   P. Edw. May England never want this training
     school
To anneal brave hearts for the rough sports of war,
When foreign danger threats our native land,
Or her own children violate her soil
With parricidal arms !   [*Exeunt.*

—— o ——

Scene 2.—*The New Forest, Hampshire.   A Forester's lodge
in a glade studded with oaks.   A brook crossed by a
foot-bridge.*

       Enter Walter *and two Foresters.*

Walter *(sings).*

     Heigh ! the merry, merry month of May,
     When the brown thrush sings,
     And the partridge springs
     From its nest in the standing hay.

Well, this is not May, or the deer might rest.   Here
is the Prince come to Farnham, and half a score of
bucks wanted for his following ; but where to find them
puzzles me.   First, there was the Abbot of Brocken-

hurst was never without a fat haunch for the refectory.
We are eaten up by priests. Then, Sir Adam Gourdon's men have scared the deer, by harbouring in the
forest. I can no longer find them in their old haunts.
I shall have to go as far as Ringwood. Look you,
Peter; you know the place where the Avon forms a
mere as it flows through the forest.

1st For. I know it well. The fourteen acre of
fern, with the copse above, and the oak wood on the
north; Hazelmere.

Walt. The very place. Go, you two, and mark
what deer have harboured in the covert. They will be
out at feed in the afternoon. I will go round by the
hill-side, and may chance to pick up an outlying hart. .
(*Exit Foresters.*) Sir Adam Gourdon is a fine fellow.
He asked me to join him. No no; I am a King's man.
To be a rebel? No, no; but I must be jogging. Ho,
Marion!

Enter Marion.

Give me my best bow and the old arrows. Old friends
are truest. Did you mend the arrow-case?

Mar. What, going again, Walter? I am always
left alone, now.

Walt. Going again? In troth am I; and to-
morrow, and the day after, and the day after that.
Let the dogs loose.

MAR. If I had married Will Draper, I had led a quiet life in the town. Here am I, left all alone in the woods, frightened out of my wits.

WALT. Tut, Marion; keep your wits to quell your fears. Will Draper, ha! ha! Call that a man, a thing of frills and ribbons, a roll of duffil, with two yard-measures across, topp'd by a coif? Marry you! marry, I pity him. A quiet life *he* would have led, the mannikin.

MAR. At least my own will I should have had.

WALT. A wretched will; a miserable will; a will-o'-the-wisp.

MAR. You flout, I don't mean that; you know I don't. I mean my own way.

WALT. The worst thing in the world for you, Marion. I am your only man; I can fight for you, and rule you too.

MAR. Don't try it.

WALT. With kisses, Marion. A woman that has her own way never knows what to do with it; but like a fool with fire, instead of hiding it to keep him warm, throws the coals about to burn all comers. A woman's will but lives by opposition, or else it dies.

MAR. There must be some one else to differ from, or there were no choice.

WALT. Just so. You shall have your will, beauty;

but I will keep it for you. Good-bye, Marion. Kiss
me. I'll be back at night, or sooner. Let Jock look
after the cows, and send Dick with the butter to Sir
Adam's quarters. I don't want his men mooning
about here; they might come for butter, and steal the
cow. Nothing is too heavy or too hot for these lads.
Come, Grip; down, Grasper. Good-bye, Marion.

MAR. Good-bye, Walter. Stay not late.

WALT. Now to meet the Prince. [*Exeunt.*

———o———

SCENE 3.—*The Forest. On one side a barn among the
trees.* PRINCE EDWARD. WALTER, *who kneels.*

P. EDW. Rise, Walter. The forest being o'errun
By Adam Gourdon's men, how is't that you
Are safe? Have you join'd this rebellious band,
And thus secured your own immunity?

WALT. No, Prince.
When—for which now I see no cause—I join
Their band, I will first give up the wages
Of the King. A true man may fairly fight
In any honest cause; but base is he
Who takes his bread from those he would betray.

E

P. Edw. Well said.   Then whence your safety,
    forester ?

Walt. My lord, Sir Adam's men have it in charge
Not to molest us ; perhaps he thinks that we
May favour them ; at least he knows full well
'Tis better have us friends than enemies.

P. Edw. And thus you go among them without
    fear ?

Walt. I do, my lord.

P. Edw.   Where are their quarters now?

Walt. Their place of gathering is the Roman
    camp,
Now fortified with palisade and trench.
A castellated ruin serves their chief
For dwelling-place ; while all around, within,
His men are hutted.   In the open glades
Outside, they're wont to practise archery ;
And I have thought no harm to join their sport,
And sometimes hit the clout.

P. Edw.   Can I trust you ?

Walt. A stranger might trust me ; my Prince,
I have to hear but and obey.

P. Edw.   Walter,
I want your help and secresy.   This day
I mean to see this rebel in his lair.
You can get me a dress like that you wear.

WALT. My lord, I can.   You will not venture it ?
'Tis very dangerous.

    P. EDW.   Is that a reason, Walter?

    WALT. Pardon.   'Twas not t' impugn your bravery,
Gallantly provèd in fair-foughten fields ;
But of more value is the Prince's life—
Fair fall the while—than those of common men.

    P. EDW. Fear not ; what is your man's name ?

    WALT. Peter, my lord.

    P. EDW. Keep him out of the way.   I'll take his
      place.
Go now : the dress.

    WALT.   I have a suit of green
Was never worn ; that will I bring your Grace.
Await me at the byre among the trees,
There you may change your garb in privacy.   [*Exit.*

    P. EDW. So late escap'd, to run this risk again !
Sheer folly ! and yet for my very life
I cannot forego this whim that's seized on me,
To penetrate the leaguer of the foe,
Unmask his game, and find out his real strength.
'Tis a sport of danger ; yet once resolv'd,
I cannot without weakness now go back.   [*Exit.*

SCENE 4.—*As before.*

Re-enter PRINCE EDWARD, WALTER.

P. EDW. So : do I look like a poor gentleman
Turn'd forester ?   Tight about the shoulders.

WALT. It will stretch in the slashing.   Few are so
   broad,
Except Sir Adam : he has grand thews.
You must bear yourself, my lord, more humbly ;
And 'twere well you join'd their camp at dusk.

P. EDW. Leave that to me.   Lack I aught out-
   wardly ?

WALT. Nothing.   But stay—forgive me if I tell
What to myself is danger ; yet I weigh not
My peril 'gainst the safety of my Prince.
Knowing the lawlessness of his own men,
The Earl a passport gave me for my need ;
For none among his reckless band would dare
Abuse his safeguard.   Here is the paper.

P. EDW. Let me see.   " For Walter the forester."
" Let the bearer pass free."   Good ; I see not how
Edward the prince can be christen'd to suit this.

WALT. My lord, it is but to cut off the name ;
'Twill suit or peer or peasant.

P. EDW. True ; and here's a scrawl—a true rebel's
   mark :
Beshrew the master that taught him to write.

It cannot be mistook. I see not though
Why I should be suspected more than you;
Because you know me, you think others must.

WALT. It may be so, my lord.

P. EDW. Listen. If I return not before morning,
you may suspect evil. Take my bugle, your warrant
to the good Knight Sir Aylmar l'Estrange, to have
a hundred lances in readiness, should force be required
for my rescue; though I doubt me the precaution is
needless. I like this garb—it is easier for fighting
than a steel case; and a man shows better in the
ladies' eyes. Now, I bethink. me, women's eyes are
sharp. Come to the lodge; I will try my new disguise
on bonny Marion.

WALT. Better not, my lord, trust a woman.

P. EDW. Ha, forester—what, jealous! that should
be tried. I will wager my dagger against your new
suit that I take a brace of kisses from her without
offence, and of her own free will.

WALT. No, my lord; it is too much honour for a
poor girl. I do not shrink from the wager; but the
best are not to be trusted with secrets.

P. EDW. Say you so? Then, by my troth, it's a
party, and the dagger is yours—win or fail. If I win,
the kisses are worth it; if I fail, it is yours by right.
And here we are.

SCENE 5.—*The same as Scene 2.*

Enter PRINCE EDWARD ; *to them* MARION.

MAR. Back again so soon, Walter? I am not sorry; but I don't want you in trouble for failing the Prince's deer. Whom have you brought? (*Aside*) A handsome youth !

WALT. Never you mind : he is a friend.

P. EDW. Beautiful Marion, this bold forester, who calls himself your lord, tells me I shall not be welcome to your roof.

MAR. Troth, will you not, Master Jack-a-napes, an' you learn not better manners : lord forsooth !— we know who is master. And you, sir, as you have learnt my name, learn further to put Mistress, in addition. A feather in your cap, too !

P. EDW. (*aside*) There, Walter, you never thought of the cap. Mistress Marion, your pardon ; you are too hard upon me ; where should a poor youth like me learn manners? But so I look on your pretty face, I care not how long you pelt me with your tongue.

MAR. And you stand by, Walter, and hear this ; you hear him praise me to my face, and do not swinge him.

WALT. Had he told a lie, and said you were not pretty, he had deserved swingeing. But you are,

Marion, and you know it; and would you have him
checked for telling the truth? Ha! ha!

MAR. O, if you take it in that way, do not blame
me if I take you at your word.

WALT. As how, Mistress?

MAR. What, are you afraid now?

P. EDW. A most sensible husband, Mistress Marion;
he likes to hear his wife praised before his face, that
she may not care for it behind his back.

MAR. And who may you be that are so pert?

P. EDW. I am the new forester; and Master Walter
here is to give me lessons in venerie. I was falconer
to a gentleman before—he gave me this cap and
feather. Now, Marion, if you will let me call you
Marion, you shall have this white feather for your own
velvet cap. Eh! Marion?

MAR. Well, as Walter does not mind, I'll take your
gift; the feather will suit my complexion.

P. EDW. It will suit your beauty, Marion. We shall
be great friends, Marion.

MAR. I' faith, soon and fast; but what is your name
first?

P. EDW. My name? O—Ed—Edwin. Aint I a
smart youth?

MAR. Not so bad to look at. Can you shoot?

P. EDW. And win. Try me.

WALT. Don't be a fool, woman. A forester, and not shoot? (*Aside*) By St. George! but she comes to the lure.

MAR. Here is a bow; now draw me a woodman's shaft. There is an antlered head nailed to yon oak, a hundred and fifty paces.

P. EDW. I am a novice yet; but give me the bow.

MAR. O, what a lovely ring! where got you it?

P. EDW. O, that—a ring of forty shillings. My master gave it me: a fair ruby. Give me your hand, Marion, to see how it looks on you. (*Puts on the ring.*) How well it looks; what a pretty hand you have!

MAR. And yours have had light work, so white as they are.

WALT. Never mind the ring, let him shoot. (*Aside*) Egad! I shall lose.

P. EDW. (*aside*) Come, Walter, that is not fair; a fair field and no favour, or I shall cry quits.

> (*As she is admiring the ring and taking it off reluctantly, he shoots wide of the mark.*)

There is an arrow lost. Keep it, Marion, now that you have worn it; I cannot take it back again.

MAR. O, Master Edwin, it is of too great value.

P. EDW. Here, Walter shall buy it for you.

WALT. Not I; I have not forty shillings in the world, barring my land.

P. EDW. I'll take less.

WALT. No; not a doit. (*Aside*) He would wing his shaft with my feather.

P. EDW. Never mind, Marion, we are friends now; and if you will not take it for nothing, you shall give me what will cost you nothing, and so there will be no obligation either way.

MAR. O! what? It is very pretty.

P. EDW. Well, it is yours; and in the way of honest courtesy — before your good man here — give me a brace of kisses. That is a cheap bargain, eh?

                    (*He shoots again and hits the mark.*)

In the clout, Walter.

WALT. (*aside*) She will not dare.

MAR. Well shot. (*Aside*) Now will I be revenged for his indifference. I don't know—well—as you are such a friend of Walter's, and he likes you to praise me, he won't mind; and as you won't take back your ring, if I must, I must. (*He kisses her.*)

WALT. (*aside*) O, the devil! I would not have believed it.

P. EDW. Lovely Marion, this is the best bargain that ever I made.   [*Exit* MARION.

Never look glum, man; 'twas a fair wager, and you have lost.

WALT. O, my lord!

P. EDW. Hush, hush!

WALT. She did not hear.

P. EDW. Talk of women blabbing! Come, there is no love lost on that venture.

Re-enter MARION *with a hunting-cap.*

MAR. Jesting apart, Master Edwin, I owe you thanks for your gifts; and see how well my cap looks with your feather.

WALT. O, vanity, vanity, a woman would not be a woman without you. Well, as long as you don't buy any more baubles with my coin, have your way.

P. EDW. Never mind him, fair Marion; when you want to buy any more rings, I am your pedlar. Lend me a bow and arrows. Is this one true?

WALT. True as a friend.

P. EDW. H'm! as friend should be, you mean.

[*Exit* PRINCE EDWARD.

WALT. Well, Mistress, have you no shame? (*Aside*) She did it without blushing.

MAR. Who is he? He had such a sweet way with him.

WALT. Sweet, call you it? The devil take such sweetness, say I; and you to ——

MAR. And so generous. Look, Walter, how it glows and sparkles. Forty shillings! It is worth more, I'm sure.

WALT. Yes, and you paid more than I like for it; my belief is he stole it.

MAR. O fie, Walter, how ungrateful; poor boy!

WALT. Boy? Cool for a youngling.

MAR. Yes, and so courteous in manner. Gentleman's service is a great polisher of your country manners. I hope he will come again.

WALT. Ay, and sell more rings. Damn it, Marion, why did you kiss him?

MAR. Ha! ha! ha! Jealous, Walter; jealous. And pray, why did you snub me before him when I complained of his flattery? Now have I been revenged, and paid you in your own coin. And I have a handsome ring into the bargain, and a feather in my cap. Ha! ha! ha!

WALT. Then you did not do it with a will?

MAR. Not I. Did I blush? Come, and I will show you the difference. (*Kisses him.*) Dear Walter!

WALT. My darling Marion, my own!   [*Exeunt.*

——o——

SCENE 6.—*The New Forest. The mound of an old Roman Camp, with embankments and ruined walls.* PRINCE EDWARD *sitting on a fallen tree, whittling a bow.*

P. EDW. A pleasant life, this, in the greenwood, if the weather were always fine, and summer all the year round; but marvellous cold work in winter.

Enter rebel cross-bowmen.

So, lads, what service have you been on?

1ST SOLD. Little service this time, save foraging for deer.

P. EDW. And not much success in that, meseems; your long-bow is your only weapon for that market.

2ND SOLD. Here is a cockerel! Who are you?

P. EDW. I am the new forester in the room of Peter.

2ND SOLD. And where is Peter?

P. EDW. Dismissed for shooting a buck in the haunch. I doubt me he used one of those arblasts. The bolt may go straight, but it's a chance; they wabble away like a frog in a current; but a well-balanc'd shaft—three-wing'd—cleaves the air like a falcon, and bites as fell.

2ND SOLD. I should not mind making a match, cross-bow against long-bow.

P. EDW. One to one is no proof, but place a thousand of the King's archers against—— how many cross-bowmen have you?

2ND SOLD. Two thousand.

P. EDW. Good—against your two thousand arbales-
tiers. They would all be spitted two deep; while their
bolts went hopping about like hail in a haystack, with
like hurt.

2ND SOLD. We have archers too.

P. EDW. Not many——

1ST SOLD. About six hundred, and as many spear-
men, with jack and sword.

P. EDW. What is your pay?

1ST SOLD. Why 'tis not much pay we get.

P. EDW. The King's men-at-arms are paid two
groats a-day, with food and shelter.

1ST SOLD. Hear that, Jenkin?

2ND SOLD. But they've no plunder.

P. EDW. No; but is it not more honourable to live
by honest gain, than like to beasts of prey? one day
full, and starved the next; as great a scourge to your
friends as to your foes; and those you deem your foes,
your countrymen. Alas! poor England, to be dis-
embowelled thus by her own children.

1ST. SOLD. He speaks truth, but here comes the
Earl.

P. EDW. I tell you, sirs, that for the long-bow there
is no wood like ash. (*Aside*) He has a hawk eye.

[*Exeunt Soldiers.*]

Enter De Gourdon.

Gour. Well, Sirrah! suppose 'tis granted—What
then?

P. Edw. Your pardon, my lord, then no more
remains.

But I am right. But 'tis not granted, sir,

For these wise choughs maintain that their cross-bows

Superior are to the long-bow and shaft.

Gour. I'm no wiser, though you've changed the
venue.

They are right, for a volley :

P. Edw.   Tut, my lord,

A bevy of quails to a string of wild geese.

Gour. Each man for his craft: you may try your
hand

Against them at the butts.

P. Edw.   Why should I so ?

For if I fail, I'm jeer'd; and if I win,

I make an enemy of each that fails.

Gour. (*aside*) His favour is familiar. Where have
I seen that face ?

Enjoy our hospitality, at least, and welcome.

P. Edw. Thanks, good my lord: I'll consort here
awhile,

And then to my own work.   [*Exit* De Gourdon.

He conn'd me close as though he knew my face.

A gallant enemy, but yet I'll try

His prowess in the field.   This position

Is well chose for a defence : the bank well lin'd

By those same cross-bowmen to gall th' attack.

A band of archers in that wood below

Methinks would drop their arrows in their waists,

And sweep them from it at three hundred paces ;

Just a sufficient rise.   That hill is bad

For an ambush ; but few knights are with him ;

Then this space—St. George ! what field for a charge !

I must join their mess, lest I awake suspicion :

Bold deeds more oft carry their own immunity.

                                        [*Exit.*

——o——

SCENE 7.—*The Rebel Camp.*

Enter ADAM DE GOURDON.

GOUR. That forester's face haunts me.   I doubt me

I grow timorous, and start at trifles.

Success has crown'd a cause more desperate

Than ours, with prudence at the helm ;

While brightest prospects have made shipwreck foul,

Wanting in due precaution.   Ho ! Wilfrid !

Fools, they say, tell the truth, and drunken men :

He is no drinker, neither is he fool :

A man in anger is akin to both,
And that bolt might hit.   Ho! Wilfrid!

Enter WILFRID.

WILF. My lord!

GOUR. Wilfrid, that forester pleases me not.

WILF. Nor me, my lord.

GOUR.　　　　　　　Wherefore! why so, Wilfrid?

WILF. A woman's reason partly,—he does not.
Then the men tell me that he says the King
Gives better pay.

GOUR.　　　Ha! did he so? indeed?—
That is against our terms of sufferance.
Listen, Wilfrid—to make him show his colours.
Put an insult on him at your board;
I will be near enough to observe him.
No blows, mind.

WILF.　　　　I see, my lord; it shall be done.

———o———

SCENE 8.—*The same.　Soldiers at mess.*　PRINCE EDWARD,
WILFRID.

WILF. That is good venison, Master Verdurer.

P. EDW. Tho' I am loth, look you, to dispraise a
man's cheer at his own board, I should say it wanted a
month of being in season.

WILF. You pretend to know woodcraft; yet you say you are new at it.

P. EDW. I said not so: new here, but bred to it.

Enter DE GOURDON *behind.*

You seem to be out of humour where there is no offence.

WILF. There is offence. I keep nought on my mind, but when 'tis there I out with it. You were heard to say that the King's men receive good wages. Now we know his men are slaves and forced to fight—torn from their homes and families: but as for pay, they do not get it—and you know they don't—and—you lied!

P. EDW. Lied! You are a brave man. I am alone, a guest; and you, surrounded by your band, insult me. You would sing another song, were you and I alone in Ringwood Close.

WILF. O never fear, you shall have fair play. A match! I'll waive my rank as captain of a band, and lend you sword and buckler.

P. EDW. I came not here to brawl. Though a forester, how know you I am not of gentle birth? And though you may waive your rank, I may not be prepared to waive mine.

WILF. The coward never wants a bush to hide his head.

P. EDW. The coward is the cock that only crows on
his own mixen.

WILF. Base-born churl!

P. EDW. Ha! Slave! (*Starts up, drawing his dirk,
and then resumes his seat.*)   He is not worth it.

GOUR. (*coming forward.*)   (*Aside*) The Prince as I
live! where were my eyes?   What brawling is this?

P. EDW. My lord, your courtesy invited me
To join your board.   But this your follower,
Your honour not regarding, mannerless,
Would drive me from it by his rudery.

GOUR. Captain, this is not treatment for a guest.

WILF. My lord, I dare affirm he is a spy.

GOUR. A spy! come hither. (*They converse apart.*)
——I have, Forester,
Ever treated you poor men with kindness.
No quarrel have I with you, but for you
Am in arms, and 'twould grieve me to believe
You would betray and violate my trust.

P. EDW. No man e'er trusted me, and was betrayed;
Where no trust is, there is no betrayal.

GOUR. Yet in important matters, it is safe
In one's own hands to keep a guarantee.
And therefore, friend, for a few days at least
I think it better you remain my guest.

P. EDW. Say your prisoner.

GOUR. You may call it so ;
And thank my forbearance, being in my power.

P. EDW. No thanks I owe you, as you trust me not :
No man has e'er distrusted my pledged word
And has not lived to sorely rue his error.

GOUR. High ground for a churl : trust you ? I might
   do so
On occasion ordinary. But this
Is business of too much weight—and I
Must take security of fortune. Follow.

    (WILFRID *with a guard of men-at-arms has sur-*
        rounded the Prince, who is led off prisoner.)
                                  [*Exeunt.*

ACT III.

SCENE 1.—DE GOURDON'S *Camp in the New Forest. A large
tent in the foreground.*

Enter HUGH DE TURBERVILLE.

TURB. O Penury !
Bleak-hearted fiend ; man might defy thy power
Standing alone. Who can support the blow,
When thy sword pierces through the hearts we love ?
O Grief ! to see the one—the one you worship—
The more than self—in whom your soul is merg'd—
For whom you thought all luxuries too harsh—

Whose foot should but on golden tissue tread
Lest the earth swell with pride, —fading away—
With drooping head—and daily weakening frame,
In all her loveliness—fading away ;—
Depriv'd at first of happiness of soul,
Then—pin'd her beauteous form by want and pain.
To see your fair child, at its mother's knee,
From the blue depths of her innocent eyes
Gazing, with frighted craving look, upon
Those glorious orbs, to heaven upraised in vain.
O agony !—can I look back—believe
This was my lot ?   I've grudg'd the broken meat
Thrown by the rich man's menial to his dog,
Knowing 'twould save my darlings from some pangs :
I've known what 'tis to covet the base coin
Given to the beggar by a pitying child.
Is't possible 'twas I, whose darken'd soul
Was by this dreadful shadow so obscur'd ?
Hast thou not, Poverty, appall'd a king !
Against thee did not Israel's King invoke
God's help ?   " Lest I be poor and steal."   And we,
Are we more perfect than this pattern-man ?
Shall man be poor now, and not steal ?   Ay, all,
All, both high and low, each in his degree
Is a stark thief ; all steal ; for bread the low ;
And for us,—what torture greater than possess

The aspirations, feelings of a prince,

And be compell'd by iron circumstance

To drag through life the beggar's sordid chain?

Enter DE GOURDON.

GOUR. Good morrow, Sir Hugh.

TURB.   Good, I would it were.

What hope is left? Our main host is dispers'd;

Its leaders slain upon the field, or dead

Upon the scaffold. With this remnant force,

How long can we withstand the kingdom's power?

GOUR. Altho' alone I stand, I will uphold

The common cause; the charter of our rights.

The fire of liberty shall still blaze high,

Though I a martyr into the pyre leap

To add new fuel to its sacred flame.

TURB. Enough for me, that I have join'd the cause.

These fine terms for motives interested

I do not—nor I care not—understand.

GOUR. Have not our ancestors shed their best
blood

To save their rights—our rights—as Englishmen?

TURB. (*aside*) English?—Gascon, Italian, Norman,
French!

GOUR. Equality before the law, free faith,

Safety of honour, life, and liberty.

TURB. And 'gainst the loaded dice we gamble still.
But did your vassals rise in the same cause,
A Norman, you would crush them for rebellion.

GOUR. The freedom they are fit for, they should have,
By wealth, by station, and intelligence.

TURB. No more of this. I fight not for posterity,
For fanciful ideas, or visioned griefs ;
But 'gainst the ulcers of the time, that eat
Into the hearts of men : the actual curse
Of wrong, injustice, suffering. O God !
Is this Thy world, and look'st Thou down on all—
On all this misery and woe—unmov'd ?

GOUR. Why rail on Providence ? cry out against
Troubles that are inherent in the world ?
The Creator should have consulted you,
His creature, how to improve creation.

TURB. Tell me, what has man done to be condemned
To suffering, and poverty, and crime ?
Say he be scourged for his proper sins,
Why born to it ?

GOUR.   'Tis meet it should be so.
A half-world you would have ; fit for a race
Of sheep, or tortoises, or zoophytes. All
That makes man noble, godlike—banish'd—
Virtue, greatness, immortality—all
A picture of the mind, invisible —

Lacking the canvas, colour, creative art,
That should show forth its glorious blazonry.

TURB.   I see not why the light should not exist
Without the darkness that now sets it off.

GOUR.   Why?   Meek-eyed Pity waits on human
      pain;
Charity, white-rob'd, soothes the wretched heart;
Forgiveness smiles on mortal injuries;
And Mercy follows on the track of Crime.
The virtues that ennoble man on earth
Are only made resplendent by great wrong:
How could fair Patience shine with placid light,
Unless there were unkindnesses,—insult,—
And all the thousand gnats of life that sting?
How, sweet Humility, with downcast look,
Finding rich jewels in the sands of earth,
But for the contumelious heel of Pride?
Glory-enhaloed Chastity would leave
The world unbeautified; but Pleasure roams
With form so fair, and meretricious brow,
And star-bespangled robe, and lustrous eyes,
Blinding the foolish ones with glittering dust.
Forgiveness, that ennobles the forgiver,
But crushes not its object, could not reign
If wolf-eyed Malice did not walk the world,
And Envy sinister, and black Revenge,

With Hatred, who but smoothes the royal road
For car-enthroned Generosity.
The great and good can only be revealed
But by their lapse.

    TURB. Meseemeth that you use high-sounding words
To justify all wickedness on earth.

    GOUR. Not so ; but were it not a sorry world,
Without these noble qualities to raise
The soul of man above his kindred earth ?

    TURB. True ; but may not these attributes exist
Without their opposites ?

    GOUR.   How were they prov'd,
Unless they had a field for exercise ?

    TURB. Evasion ! Truth absolute, and purity, and
      good
Should stand alone—self-pois'd.

    GOUR.   Then were we Gods,
And all this beauteous frame of universe
Had not emerg'd from dark, nor man been made.
All that is not God must be imperfect,—
Hence evil in the world, and Satan's fall !

    TURB.   Babbling philosophy !
Descend to earth. Against the oppressions
Of the King and Legate have we fought—and lost.

    GOUR. Was this not cause to move a noble spirit
To remedy their sad misgovernment,

And place more power in the Barons' hands,
To check, control this rampant tyranny?

TURB. That is not acting on your theory
Of virtuous meekness and humility;
May *we* not to so high a pitch aspire?

GOUR. I justified the ways of Providence;
But man 'gainst evil must for ever strive,
The evil which attacks his inward soul,
And violation of the public rights.

TURB. For the public? my cause was private wrong:
My heritage—my land—was confiscate:
I play'd for equal stakes, and have lost all.
They were the stronger and they crushed us:
Had we been victors, we had been reveng'd.
'Tis the rule of life: to the stronger—gain
And triumph; to the weaker—loss and ruin.

GOUR. Alas for England, if all thought like you!
I deem'd your motives higher.

TURB. I thought you wiser.

GOUR. The peasants for their hire serve, or spoil;
But even they have faith in freedom's rights.

TURB. Pshaw! they've faith iu empty stomachs.
There never was rebellion yet on earth
That was not born of squalid poverty,
Though nurs'd by wild ambition. Poverty!
How few of our rank know what that means!

A fiend that forces man his honour sell ;
Woman, her sanctity—her soul—for bread,
Or for the means of life.

    Gour.   Better to die.

    Turb.   'Tis easy said : failing experience—
Dire experience—you cannot judge.

    Gour.   Worse trials I can image to my mind.

    Turb.   Imagination cannot grasp the facts.
I had a wife and child ; they died of want ;
They died—both died ; my heav'n, my all, was lost;
And all the world became to me a blank.

    Gour.   Is it possible ?   I deeply feel for you.

    Turb.   Enough of this.   What are your present
       plans ?

    Gour.   They are bright with promise.   I would have
       told you
But for this argument—that I hold the Prince
A prisoner.

    Turb.   The Prince ?   Where ?   How comes it
I heard not of it ?

    Gour.   It was but to-day
He came disguised—alone—and was discovered.

    Turb.   And is now here ? (*aside*) out of this—) in
       your camp ?

    Gour.   Yes.   Why muse you ?   A noble vantage-
       ground
Does this afford for peaceful terms, or war.

TURB. (*aside*) To me a ground whereon to build
my fortunes.

GOUR. You are thoughful, Sir Hugh.

TURB.   Thoughtful ? I was—
Yes; I was musing how this happy chance
Might fashion'd be by wisdom such as yours,
To balance our unequal armaments,
And cause the weaker triumph.

GOUR.   Come in with me;
We'll talk of this at length.

TURB.   But who guards him?
The temptation for common men is great :
Might I advise—forgive me—caution ?

GOUR. 'Tis well provided for; come in with me.

TURB. Yet I feel anxious ; I will follow you.

                        [*Exit* DE GOURDON.

Poor fool! too good for this world, where only thrive
Injustice and high-handed robbery—
Shall I add treachery ? well, 'twill give him
A mean to practise his bald theories
Of humility and tame forgiveness,
Bear out his argument, and let him prove
How easier far it is to talk than suffer.   [*Exit*.

SCENE 2.—*A Vaulted Chamber.* PRINCE EDWARD. *He sits down musing, then breaks into a fit of laughter.*

P. EDW. After all, it is no laughing matter;
Yet laughable it is to be cag'd thus.
How often do we feel a consciousness
Of safety when surrounded by great peril;
A trace, perchance, of man's prophetic spirit
Remaining from the fall.
I marvel did he know me? He was calm:
I marked his words were temper'd by respect.
There would for a forester have been threats
Of whipping, or of worse. He knows me, then.
But why am I immured? There is a cause.
He would not dare approach my life;
He is too wise to brave the consequence.
Patience! I see it all; he'll keep me here
Until he has o'erthrown my force—unchief'd.
Escape I must; but how? A solid vault:
Famous builders were these ancient Romans.
It can be but a shell; yet the whole depth
Of the mound is over it. A grating
I see, which may reveal a weaker point.
Some one comes.

[*Enter a Guard with food.*

Well, comrade, how much longer
Am I to be shut up in this dark hole?

SOLD. As long as the Earl pleases; until your time
comes for heading or hanging.

P. EDW. I would speak with him; pray tell him so.

SOLD. Tell him, quotha! Not I; he is busy mus-
tering his troops, and can't attend to such as you.

P. EDW. (*aside*) I thought as much—When does
he march?

SOLD. How should I know? Here he is. [*Exit.*

Enter SIR ADAM DE GOURDON, *in armour.*

GOUR. This comedy must end. Prince! I know you.

P. EDW. Ha! you know me; yet there you stand,
and bend not
Your vassal-knee to our supremacy.

GOUR. You forget; supremacy and power
Are mine by fortune's favour. It were better
By concessions to buy your perill'd life,
Than strive for baseless ceremonies.

P. EDW. I forget nothing. I forget not your
treason;
Less can I forget myself, or the dignity
Of my father's crown. How base is that man
Whose nature can be chang'd by circumstance.
The mail makes not the knight; nor coat of frieze
The peasant. I am thy Prince—my vassal thou;

And this no form nor circumstance can alter :
Then 'tis for you to sue, and me to hear.

    Gour. I am your peer, Sir Prince, but let that pass ;
Our grievances, for which we took up arms,
Are known to you ; yet you deny redress
And justice.   Are you prepared to treat for——

    P. Edw. Treat ?   I, while your prisoner ?   Open
      those doors ;
Resume your proper place : submit yourself
And all your followers to our clemency ;
Then to your suit may we incline our ear.

    Gour. So, you brave me; you yet may learn what 'tis
To press a desperate man.   Wilfrid, what ho !
It were scant wisdom to spare one, a foe
So bitter, the head of our opposers.

              Enter Wilfrid.

Bring the tortures.

    P. Edw.   Vassal, thou durst not !
If my life you seek, take it ; I care not ;
But insult me not.   I am still your Prince.

    Gour. Not that I dare not ; but it were unmeet,
And would let wrath usurp the place of reason.
Wilfrid, order the headsman to attend,
And be you ready at my call.   [*Exit* Wilfrid.
My lord, I offer you your life : for which,
My lands and goods restored, my followers

Pardoned, the people's grievances redress'd,

And——

   P. Edw. Hold! I spurn your offer, as I spurn

    yourself.

Were I so base as make such terms with you

Upon compulsion, they could never bind

The conscience of the King.   But I disdain

This subterfuge, unworthy of my place,

And honour's dignity.

   Gour.   Know you, Sir Prince,

Your head, carried before my van, were worth

Ten thousand men, to terrify our foes;

Your army then half-conquer'd by dismay,

Would fall an easy prey.

   P. Edw.   Sir Knight, thou dream'st!

Didst thou dare

To touch with sacrilegious hands our life,

No terror would it cause, but would raise up

The horrent spirit of a dire revenge,

So potent, universal through the land,

That, like a feather in the storm, the regicide

Would vanish from the earth.

   Gour.   You little know

How small a space the greatest fill on earth.

Too many interests there are in life

For men to care—once gone—for a dead prince.

His life's a pebble thrown into a pool;
A ripple, a few bubbles on the surface,
And over it the waters close, as though
It had not been; while no man misses it.
So prepare.

    P. Edw.   I dare sooner die, than you
Dare do the deed.   Once more, Sir Knight, beware!
    Gour. There are few things I dare not.   I laugh at
      fear;
Nought I lose, and may gain all.

    P. Edw.   Yes, infamy.
    Gour. Infamy!   (*aside*) My heart yearns to him,
      and yet my safety.

          Enter Wilfrid, *and takes him apart.*

    Wilf. My lord, I cannot trust the guard.
    Gour.   Why so?
Or is it yourself that quails?

    Wilf. Have I ever fail'd you?   But the men,—as yet
they know nothing; but, should the Prince proclaim
himself, no man will lay a hand upon his life.   And,
doubtless, he will appeal to their allegiance.

    Gour. 'Tis better so.   Yes, Wilfrid; I fear it is so.
Nor did I wish to touch his life, but work upon his
fears, and so obtain our ends.   We must now dissemble;
and, holding him a hostage, we may make terms
honourable with the King, when we have, in his absence,
defeated the forces he has brought against us.

P. Edw. When you have done, you and your villein, with your whisper'd treason, may we know its purport?

Gour. Sir Prince, the news he brings may render unadvisable my threatened step. A prisoner you remain, until releas'd under my hand, if all goes well; if not, expect a harder durance.

P. Edw. Take my defiance. But once free, look to't. This treatment shall be bitterly aveng'd.
Look to it!

Gour.   I can well afford to brave it.
Not without reason have I drawn the sword,
Nor will I sheathe it without honour gained.   [*Exit.*

—— o ——

Scene 3.—*The New Forest.* De Gourdon's *camp.*
Enter De Gourdon, Wilfrid.

Gour. The tide which turned against me has flowed
      back,
And landed me upon this rock of vantage.
The Prince for hostage, we may dictate terms;
And if the enemy refuse, we still
May fight, and 'gainst a headless host, seize victory.
Our force array'd at once we'll take the field.

Wilf. My lord, they wait the signal to set forth.

Gour. Is the vault strongly guarded?

G

WILF.   It is so ;

And his hands are scarcely made for mining.

We needs must conquer, or expect all deaths ;

For after this day's work there is no hope

Of mercy if we fall into their hands.

GOUR. What orders have you given to the guard ?

WILF. To treat him well ; but only to release

On written order, with your manual sign.

GOUR. They must not know whom they have got in
    ward ;

A trial 'twere to their fidelity.

Servility is princes' parasite.

WILF.   They know it not.

GOUR.   As soon as we have reached

Our nightly bivouac, spread wide the news,

To cheer our soldiers' hearts.   The absent Prince

Will thus fight with them, on our side.   Away !

                                     [*Exeunt.*

——o——

SCENE 4. — *The Vault.*

PRINCE EDWARD.

P. EDW. So all is quiet, and the hum has ceased

Of voices, and the sough of many feet.

All is silent, save the sentry's tramp,

And cricket's shrilling note, that pierces clear

And painfully through the dark solitude.

My patience is exhausted; but caution:

He cannot reach my camp before the morn;

Walter I can trust to bring me rescue,

But dread the loss of time. Were I once free,

Short time would it take to ride before

And counteract his plans. I have my dirk,

If I should be compell'd to force my way;

But first for other means (*Knocks at the door*).

What, ho! the guard!

SOLD. (*without*) What want you, with this noise?

P. EDW.   What is the hour?

SOLD. Ten, by the dial, if the sun shone at night.

P. EDW. Say to your captain I would speak with him.

SOLD. I will tell him so, Master Forester.

Enter Captain.

CAPT. Now, sirrah, what have you to say?

P. EDW.   Thus much:

I marvel I am kept so long in durance;

All your forces having march'd away,

No further cause exists for my detention.

CAPT. I understand you not.

P. EDW. What are your orders?

CAPT. A question for a prisoner!

P. EDW.   I will tell you.

When the Earl quitted me he said, that being on an

expedition of some weight, and F might carry informa-

tion to forestall his plans, he could not trust me;
therefore, until upon his march, I should be kept a
prisoner. He is now gone. Is this true?

CAPT. Though it were, you still remain, until I have
better warrant for your leave.

P. EDW. What token did he give you for my release?

CAPT. I may now tell you. You stay until an
order I receive, under the Earl's hand, to set you free.

P. EDW. I am content. I think 'tis now about the
hour of ten. By that order (*giving a paper*) you are
relieved from your trust. He is my noble master, and
would do no hurt to a poor man; though faith, he
might have trusted me.

CAPT. (*reads*) " Let the bearer pass free at ten :"
and his name, true enough. You are free.

P. EDW. Give me my bow; I will not go without
my bow.

CAPT. You might rejoice to go with a whole skin;
but you are free.

(Signs to the guard, who brings the bow, &c.)

P. EDW. Thanks, good captain. I owe you a service.

(He is going out.)

Enter SIR HUGH DE TURBERVILLE.

TURB. Stop! By whose orders is your prisoner free?

P. EDW. Sir Hugh de Turberville! we've met before.

TURB. Yes; that time to my cost; but now to yours.

CAPT. My orders were to keep my prisoner

Until releas'd under the Baron's hand.

There is the discharge. (*Giving the paper.*)

TURB. This?

P. EDW.   Why do you smile?

TURB. I should have thought an order of this import
Would first of all set forth the holder's name.
Captain, you are cozen'd.   Then see you not
This paper, said to have been writ to-day,
Is soil'd and rumpled with a three months' wear.
Captain, you are cozen'd ; you may rejoice
That I return'd in time to rescue you
From your lord's vengeance.

    P. EDW. (*aside*) Caught at the rebound ; here's an
      outer net.

You'll not deny the pass is from the Earl?

    TURB. But I deny the pass is for the——.   No ;
Confess you picked it up in the forest.
Captain, you are relieved of your charge,
I will examine the prisoner alone.   [*Exit Captain.*

    P. EDW. (*aside*) I know this man, and think I have
      his clue,
Else he's a fool to trust me with his life.

    TURB. De Gourdon's mind misgave him that his
      guard
Was scarcely fitted for so high a trust,
And might be overreach'd.   I came in time

To justify his apprehension, Prince,
And thwart your plans.

P. Edw.   (*aside*) Now could I strike him down
Like a leveret; better if I can
Avoid all violence.

Turb.   You said but now
That we had met before; yes, more than once,
And ever as my evil genius, Prince,
With ruin and destruction in your train.

P. Edw.   I hold me free from personal enmity.
You're one of those who joined the Barons' league,
And fell with them; your lands were confiscate
By the Privy Council to the state; not——
Enough, Sir Knight, you have me in this cage:
What is your price?

Turb.   Not so loud; shall I sell
My revenge?

P. Edw.   Your revenge! Man, you're a fool.
Revenge yourself on fortune. I know not
The Englishman I am not friends withal,
The fighting done. None beaten in fair fight
Should malice bear.

Turb.   And is't not malice
To pursue the vanquish'd with these penalties?

P. Edw.   No; to deprive your foes of power to harm
No malice is, but needful policy.
Return, Sir Knight, to your allegiance!

Not for vain boast—hear this for argument,—
I've triumphed o'er the Earl of Leicester
And all his banded nobles—crush'd them ;
And shall this freebooter stand up alone,
And brave the majesty of England's throne
Without a check ?—Leave, while it is yet time,
A ruin'd cause.   From me you may expect
Clemency ; but if into the King's hands
You vanquish'd fall—justice without mercy.

TURB.   Clemency !
A princely offer to a ruin'd man !

P. EDW.   No offer, but a warning. Stay ! speak not,
Nor dictate what I may not choose to hear.
Sir Hugh, I offer your estates restor'd,
Your seat of Ashburn Fells, and all the lands
Thereto appurtenant.

TURB.   With free pardon ?

P. EDW.   With a free pardon, on my princely word.

TURB.   (*kneels*)   I seal my fealty on your royal hand.

P. EDW.   (*aside*)   He's not the only man who has
    his price ;
'Tis of such stuff conspirators are made,
Not patriots.—How may we pass the guard ?

TURB.   They are relieved already by my men
In expectation of this issue, Prince.

P. EDW.   (*aside*)   A smooth traitor !—Then on ; lead
    on the way.   [*Exeunt.*

SCENE 5.—*Night. The Field.* DE GOURDON'S *men bivouacked.*

Enter DE GOURDON, WILFRID, *Knights and Officers.*

GOUR. Near upon four miles, you say?

WILF. Yes, four miles we've come.

GOUR. Are the men rested, and all stragglers join'd?

WILF. All are come up, except De Turberville.

GOUR. I have employed Sir Hugh on other duty,
For double surety of the captive Prince.

WILF. You have?—that is indeed to set the fox
To guard the honest guardian of the sheep.

GOUR. How? do you suspect him? he hates the Prince
For all he has lost and suffered; doubt you
His loyalty?

WILF. No, but I doubt his need:
A man who only fights for what he's lost
Will turn against you but to gain it back:
Like cats, my lord, they have no love for man,
But only follow food. But who comes here?

Enter a Peasant.

GOUR. Whence are you?

PEAS. I come from the Prince's camp
Now pitch'd within a league from where you stand.
A strange commotion reigns there; no man sleeps;

The hum of voices and the clash of arms

Drown all the midnight voices of the woods.

I came to warn you, as the people's friend.

GOUR. So near! this thwarts my plans; I like it not;

The hive has lost its queen : but this advance

Was unexpected. Surprise is useless ;

We must regain the shelter of our trench,

And there await the attack which they intend.

The dawn approaches : countermarch the men;

While with some knights I ride to offer terms.

[Exeunt.

———o———

SCENE 6.—*The Field.* PRINCE EDWARD'S *camp entrenched.*

Enter to the barriers, ADAM DE GOURDON *and knights,*
with a HERALD, *on horseback.*

GOUR. Go, herald, sound a parle: summon their
Chief

The leader of their troops to conference.

(*The* HERALD *advances, and blows a blast, which is*
answered from the other side. Enter within
the barrier PRINCE EDWARD *and attendants,*
mounted. The Prince in armour, with a
crowned helmet.)

P. EDW. What warlike challenge wakes this early
hour?

Gour. Sir Knight, this jugglery is out of place :
It needs not you should thus usurp the form—
The outward form of royalty—the Prince
Being my prisoner ; for whose release
I come to make such terms, as may become
My honour and your straits.　Say, you refuse—
I go to seize advantage at the flood,
And take perforce what is denied to faith.
My men, all eager for the fray, await
In confidence to be led forth against
Your headless host.

    P. Edw.　　　　　　　Presumptuous vassal !
That dar'st thus rashly to approach our presence,
And bargain for our freedom with ourself.
'Twere more becoming than expound such terms,
That you and your confederates should sue
To us for life, with halters round your necks.
You'd sell the lion's hide ; beware his fangs ;
And let the lion sitting on this crest
Daunt your rebellious hearts.

    Gour.　Could large-mouth'd words stand in the
       place of proof,
Yours would be worthy of your outer case ;
But not of that poor garb of yesterday,
In which the true Prince aped humility.

Enough of this : I hold your Prince in durance ;
'Tis not a crested helm can make another.

    P. EDW. That crown-wreathed helm was never doff'd
    —nor now—

To traitors. But lo, to unnerve thine arm,
And cast pale fright among thy followers :

                           (*He raises his visor.*)

Behold ! despair thy craft—and tremble.

    GOUR. Fury ! By all that's sacred, 'tis the Prince !
O treachery, dark-working fiend, that lov'st
To thwart the labours of the subtle brain,
What power has man against thy deadly guile !
The highest aims, the noblest plans work'd out
By all the patient efforts of the mind,
Are at the mercy of thy smiling face ;
A serpent foe that in man's bosom lies,
And gnaws the life strings of the very heart,
That cherish'd it within its inmost core.

    P. EDW. Rail not on treachery ; arch traitor thou !
Rather despise your one-eyed foolishness
That blindly plots and plans, and never deems
That other men have wits to countermine
Your shallow artifice. Think you your Prince
So dull a fool, as to sit by and watch
Your toils enfold him, did he not well know
Such spiders' webs were swept away at will.

Well might our subjects scorn allegiance
To such a helpless head.   You came to strike,
For so you thought, a blow against our forces
Unprepar'd.   In our turn, we offer you
Your pardon to obtain from the King's grace,
Upon your free surrender.   Refuse it,
And before to-morrow's sun shall red
The eastern clouds, the shrinking earth shall glow
With redder dyes from many a rebel's heart.
You are protected by the law of arms.
Away ; submit to the King's clemency
Before too late ; our pow'r let slip
Shall force you to obedience.   [*Exeunt.*

——o——

ACT IV.

Scene 1.—*The New Forest. One side of* De Gourdon's *camp attacked by* Aylmar l'Estrange *with the King's forces.*

Enter De Gourdon, Aylmar l'Estrange, Robert Leyburn.

Gour. Bravely done, my merry men ; shoot close.
The day is ours ; they fly : forward !
England and liberty !

> (*The King's troops are repulsed.* Aylmar, *trying to rally them, encounters* De Gourdon, *and after a short fight is cut down.*)

Gour. The Prince's friend! poor youth; if I had
time
I'd grieve for you: my sword weeps for the piteous
deed. [*Exeunt.*

———o———

Scene 2.—*The other side of the camp.*

Enter Prince Edward, *Knights and forces. He
dismounts.*

P. Edw. Hot work, gentlemen, for an autumn morn.
Our beaten foes have left the open field,
And shut themselves within their fenced camp;
From whence—but first we must hear how have fared
Our comrades on the other side. Here comes
One, to whose spirit wing'd his horse's speed
Seems slow.
Enter Robert Leyburn, *wounded.*
Say, in brief, what news?
Leyb. Prince, then thus:
Storming the camp upon the eastern side
Our men were driven back. Sir Aylmar,
Defeat disdaining, forward rode to rally
His fainting troops; again the strife was join'd.
'Twas then De Gourdon in the mingled war
Encounter'd him. Death on his helm sat crown'd:
Twice did the puissant Earl lower his sword,
As loth to ruinate so fair a form;

Sir Aylmar, like a seraph arm'd to smite
The arch-fiend—flew upon his foe, recoiled
Against his strength as 'gainst a rock—again
Dar'd the assault, confiding in his skill.
All vain ; short was the strife.   I strove to reach
The combatants, forgetful of myself ;
Press'd on ; receiv'd this wound ; and then he fell.

   P. Edw. O grief !

   Leyb.   I reach'd the spot, and rais'd his head ;
He tried to speak : I loos'd his helm—a word—
A few words he spoke—" My Prince—brother—love,"
And that was all.   Then with a happy smile,
As one that sleeps, he clos'd his eyes and died.

   P. Edw. Brother ! yes, he lov'd me more than brother.
O, I could weep—but no—away soft tears ;
Hover avenging lightnings on my steel,
And let him feel before he sees the blow,
That falls in thunder on the doomed crest
Of his rebellious head.   Dear friend, I come
Too late to save, but not too late to avenge.
So help me heaven—thy blood upon thy foe ;
Or should I fail ; O not too late to die—
To die, and overtake thy happy soul,
Winging its painless flight to paradise.
To horse ! Away ; and check this rising tide.

                              [*Exeunt.*

SCENE 3.—*Another part of the field.*

PRINCE EDWARD *and Forces. The rebel soldiers defending the entrenched camp.*

P. EDW. Shame on ye, soldiers ! will ye fly before

A scum of villeins, and half-clothed outlaws,

That, acorn-fed till now, have hid themselves

In woods and brakes ?   Shame on ye !   The beadles

From the neighbour towns would fright such rogues.

On, gentlemen—for shame—follow your Prince,

Or see him fall like a true Englishman,

Alone, unconquered !   Away with cross-bows !

In line, level your spears, St. George for England !

Charge !   Victory !

> (*They drive the enemy from their defences.*
> PRINCE EDWARD, *leading, leaps his
> horse over the barrier into the rebel
> camp, followed by his knights.*)

(*Scene changes to the interior of the camp.* PRINCE EDWARD
and followers on one side. DE GOURDON *and his force on
the other.*)

P. EDW. Hold ! let a bugle sound ; the fighting cease ;

While I and this arch rebel close the war

By our two single arms.

> (*Trumpet sounds a recall.*)

Turn, Baron, turn :

Spare we these caitives' lives.

GOUR. Well met ; and God decide the right !

P. Edw. St. George for England !

Gour. England and freedom !

> (*They charge with spears, the* Prince *is*
> *unhorsed and the* Earl's *horse is thrown.*
> *They continue the fight on foot with*
> *battle-axes. After a severe struggle,*
> *the* Earl *is struck down and disarmed.*)

P. Edw. Now yield thee, prisoner; rescue or no
rescue ;

Or die the death !

Gour. I yield to thee—my honour sav'd.

P. Edw. Hardly your life.

Gour. I ask it not ; but for some little space
To disengage me from the ties of earth,
And school my spirit for a better world.

P. Edw. Proclaim our victory ; let no more blood
Be shed ; more than enough already
On this quarrel. Keep him close prisoner.

[*Exeunt.*

———o———

Scene 4.—*A hall of state.*

Enter Prince Edward *attended.* De Gourdon *brought*
in, in chains.

Gour. Why this suspense ? unless it be t' increase
The bitterness of death ?

P. Edw.   Say it were so !

Gour. The victory is yours, and yours to use it
According to your pleasure.

P. Edw.   Or rather
According to your deserts.   Rebellion
What pretext strong can justify?   What plea
Ward off the justice of the broken law?
Or breathe of mercy for your forfeit life?

Gour. Prince, I expect it not.   I have lost all;
And like a ruin'd gambler, I care not
Though my life my fortunes follow.   Plead? yes,
Somewhat I could to save it; but wherefore?
You would not understand me on that theme:
I can but now fulfil my destiny.
Smooth the world-mill goes round, amid the crash
Of the universe's enginery:
Giant-fang'd with pestilence, pleasure, war,
Famine, and heat, and cold and accidents,
And fed with souls and bodies of our race.
All feelings lacerate, affections marr'd;
All worldly interests, fortunes, friendships,
Loves, all—all torn asunder crush'd and rent
By its remorseless adamantine teeth:
Yet still the world-mill goes round—regardless
As it rolls what it winnows, wounds, or saves;
Yet with unerring purpose it divides
The good and bad.   Man vainly strives to 'scape

H

Its vortex wide, which surely draws him in,
To wring his heart or brain with suffering,
And cast him forth at last—or purified
As heavenly seed, meet for the fields of bliss,
Or winnow'd chaff drifted on fickle winds,
To be consumed by the fires of hell.

    P. Edw. Man's will can stay it. Man is not the slave
Of fate or destiny.   To him was given
Dominion over all things from the first.

    Gour. Yes? Let me see thy power ; with a torch,
Or with a city's conflagration
Darken the sun ; arrest the raging storm
Engulphing the lone ship ; or stay one hour
The rising tide.   Thy power cannot prevent
The forming of one little drop of rain.

    P. Edw. Yet have I power on your life.   The axe
That waits without will prove your reasoning false.

    Gour. 'Twill prove it true.   Think you to stop the
       wheels
Of the universe? who on them are but—dust !
Mov'd by so slight a wind—as anger—
Or revenge—if that name names your weakness ?
No—still roll on th' inexorable wheels :
One grain another crushes in the crowd,
Ground in the daily round ; the larger grains

A little longer to the surface rise,
But that is all.   The slayer and the slain
Are but the units of a congruous whole.

   P. Edw.   Your taunt is just; yet is the strong the
     lord
Of time's events; the weak alone are crush'd
By circumstance; for passion's master soars
Above the jarring vortex of the world,
And is not subject to its accidents.

   Gour.   Where is the man so calm—so passionless—
That can stand up amid the hurtling strife
Of this bad human world unmov'd by fear,
By interest, by pride, revenge or love?
Where is the man immoveable, when all
His hopes are crush'd; sever'd his dearest ties;
His enemies triumphant; nothing left
For him—but to take stand on that lone point,
His magnanimity; and smile serene,
Rock-bas'd while sweep around ten thousand storms.
Yea, such a man—so firm, so passionless—
Might, like a huge diamond rock, cast in,
Check the wheels, and be master of the world !
There are none such; the base are slaves of gain
And passions low; the high are slaves of pride,
Ambition, fame; your masters still : slaves all.
You are not free !   You cannot even rule

The little realm that lies within your heart,
Yet you would rule the world.

    P. Edw.   You know not
What I can do.

    Gour. You dare not let me live.

    P. Edw. Your life is forfeit to the outrag'd laws.

    Gour. They're easy satisfied. But O, how hard
To atone for wounded pride. Can you forget
Your threaten'd vengeance, late my prisoner?
I repent me not that then I spar'd you ;
Too well I know that such an injury
Is not to be forgiven ; nor can you
Forgive it.

    P. Edw.   O yes ! yours was the fortune
Of the hour. To-day she has made amends.
Such vicissitudes are outward, forgiv'n
Easily, and affect not the fix'd soul.
You found no suppliant. I was still your Prince.

    Gour. Can you forgive the arduous, long campaign,
Through which we strove, and held our liberty,
Despite your power, while Leicester was a king
As great as Henry ? 'Tis something to have fought for.

    P. Edw. This rather craves my thanks ; but lessens
      not
Your guilt. Experience and age made him
And you the better leaders in the field.
The greater is my triumph now to add

Your laurels to the garland on my brow,

Which, but for your valiant stand, had faded,

And dropp'd its wan leaves in the lap of peace.

GOUR. This mock humility deceives me not.

Doubtless it is—yes, easier 'tis to bear

General defeat, that falls on all alike,

Than personal and individual loss.

Condoned all else, the death of Aylmar yet

Demands, I know, my life's due penalty.

He was your friend—you pale :—so let me pass

To my seal'd doom. Delay is double death.

P. EDW. Madman, forbear ! Retire, gentlemen.

Leave us alone.

(*The attendants retire to the back of the scene.*)

(*Aside*) 'Tis true. How I loved him !

Aylmar ! the man whose sword is crimsoned

With thy dear blood, now stands within my pow'r,

That blood which calls upon me for revenge

From all thy " dumb-mouth'd " wounds. Hear me,

    dear friend ;

O, let thy generous spirit come to me.

Descend ! and teach mine how a Prince should act.

GOUR. Prince, 'tis in vain—beyond the pow'r of

    man

To pardon such a deep offence as this.

Leave me to my fate. Me you have conquer'd;

Harder to conquer self.

P. Edw. (*aside*) I will be firm ; yet, O how high the
    price !
But England can ill spare so great a man.
Yes, you slew my friend ; and I fain would prove
My love for him—killing your life for his.
'Twould be but righteous justice, not revenge.
But lo ! his noble form I see arrest,
With action dignified, the headsman's sword,
Upraised ; and soft, my spirit hears his voice,
" Nobly I fell, in honourable war ;
Dishonour not my tomb with knightly blood."
And though most hard this deadly injury,
I can—yes, though most hard—I can forgive.
    Gour. (*aside*) Noble youth !   I can find it in my heart
To love you.   Alas, there is more behind
Which I scarce dare approach ; yet it must come.
Better from me than from his wounded soul.
Dangers are lesser, fac'd by the bold heart.——
I know not which to honour most in you,
Your love for your lost friend, whose fate I weep,
Or the great conquest, if not counterfeit,
Over your spirit gain'd.   I've not yet done—
(*aside*) (I see the conflict of his soul ; but on)—
For there remains one great—may I not say
Unpardonable—wrong, which never yet
Did aught but blood atone.   Do you not guess ?
    P. Edw. (*aside*) God help me to bear this with fortitude.

GOUR. Or rather, is it not the one great cloud
That weighs upon your soul, and urges it
To havoc and revenge ?   How easy, then,
Hurt pride, friends' blood, lost glory to forgive,
Reserving the dread thunderbolt of wrath
To fall in one accumulated blow
Upon the rival of a thwarted love.—
Margaret !

   P. EDW. No more !   Guards, ho ! to me !   Strike
     off his chains !
You are free !

      (*The guard lead off* DR GOURDON, *and exeunt.*)

—o—

SCENE 5.—*An Apartment.*

Enter PRINCE EDWARD.

   P. EDW. Thank God, 'tis done: this agony will leave
A sweeter rest hereafter.   This trial
I greatly dreaded, but I knew must come.
O what a warfare is a man's with self !
A dead lock—self against self !   On one side
Are all the passions and some virtues too ;
Justice and love and friendship side by side
With jealousy, revenge and suffering :
On the other some attributes of God,

Mercy, generosity and pity.

But by His sovran help in this fell strife

I've prov'd victorious : yet I feel as one

Just sav'd from drowning, still faint; but who comes ?

Enter MARGARET (*wildly*).

MARG. Pardon ! oh pardon ! Prince—once more

I throw me at your feet to sue for life—

For life—his life ; dearer to me than mine.

P. EDW. Had you come sooner, lady ——

MARG.   O, no ! no !

Say not I am too late : save—O save him !

I will be yours—nothing will I refuse—

Take *my* life—let *me* be your slave ; but save—

Save him, my own, my best beloved—save—Oh !

(*She faints and is supported by the Prince.*)

P. EDW. My trial it seems is not yet over.

If I took her at her word ; no, not so ;

I love her far too much to injure her.

Lady, look up, he's safe.   How beautiful !—

If this lasts ——

MARG. (*reviving*) He is dead.   Did you not say

It was too late ?

P. EDW.   No, he lives.

MARG.   Are you sure ?

O do not mock me—it were cruel of you :

You once said—you lov'd me—you would not—

No, you would not make me suffer : for if—
If you lov'd me—you would suffer with me,
Seeing my grief.   And have you pardoned him?

   P. EDW. I have ; but should have found the task
      more hard,
Had you been by.   Yet have you not promis'd
That if his life were saved you would be mine?

   MARG. 'Tis true : I said it—I will keep my word.
I will not cavil on the fact, that you
Had pardon'd him already, ere I came ;
Nor plead my woman's terrors.   For my love—
It is not mine.   Only I am your thrall.
God help *him* to bear it.   Women are born
To suffer.   My word is pass'd, 'tis sacred.

   P. EDW. Nobly spoken, lady, but, by my faith,
Had you not lost your wits, I had not gained
Your plighted word.   No matter, you are mine,
To be dispos'd of at my will.   Is't so?
You hear me not!

   MARG.   He will curse me!   O God!
What have I done? thought him so vile—that he
Will save his life by sacrifice of mine !

   P. EDW. Lady, you shall have no cause to repent.
Be calm ——

   MARG.   I—O yes—very calm.   Mock not
My misery : he comes.   I dare not meet him.

P. Edw. If you would but hear.

Marg.   I know not what I said.

O hide me from him.

P. Edw.   Hear reason—listen——

Marg. No—no—no—(*Tries to rush out, the Prince
    detains her.*)

                Enter De Gourdon.

Gour. Ha, Margaret!   What means this ?

P. Edw.   Let me speak.

This lady is my property ; at least

What may be seen of her ; she gave herself

A ransom for your life ; and being mine

To do with as I please, I give her you :

Though valueless to me, a heartless hand,

On you no richer gift could I bestow,

For love goes with it.

Gour.   Noble Prince !

P. Edw.   Take her,

She is yours—all yours.

Marg.   Is this true ?   O joy !

Gour. Kneel, Margaret, with me.

The heart that never bow'd to man before

Now bows to thee, for thou hast conquered me ;

Not by thy sword, that can but kill or hurt

The weaker flesh, leaving the spirit free.

But thou hast vanquish'd in a nobler war ;

True victory ! disarm'd the mind, and bound
My spirit to thy magnanimity.
(*Rising*) Worthy thou art to rule o'er noble hearts,
That can so bravely trample on thine own.
My life—'tis something—and I thank thee for it;
But thou hast given me more, far more; thou hast
Given me to believe in human greatness.
Accept my homage, Prince.　Never again
Can my firm faith and loyalty e'er swerve
From one so great, the ruler of himself.
　P. Edw.　And I have gain'd a friend.
　Gour.　　　　　For life and death !

Scene closes.

LOVE AND HATE.

An Allegory.

"Like a star disorb'd."—SHAKSPEARE.

Dramatis Personæ.

CHRYSES, *Christian Prince of Antioch.*

SYLVIOLA, *the Wood-Spirit.*

SATAN.

THE ANGEL.

A FIEND.

AZRAEL, *the Angel of Death.*

LOVE AND HATE.

AN ALLEGORY.

———◆·◆———

SCENE 1.—*Hell.* SATAN *seated on a diamond throne, in a vast hall of gloom, lighted by an horizon of lurid fire, attended by the infernal princes and powers.* SYLVIOLA *descends to solemn music.*

SYL. All hail! great Prince!

SAT.　　　　　What brings thee to these shades
Like a bright ray, fair daughter, 'thwart the gloom?
For fair thou art, as shell-borne Ashtaroth,
Whose worship slew great Kings in Israel.
And well might'st thou, as she did, overthrow
The chosen ones ; whom I would willing plunge
Within these fires.　But sorrowful you seem ;
The cause? Speak : is there aught we can deny
That one so fair can ask ?

SYL.   Ever the theme !

O ! bait for mortal women ! be they vile,

Or ignorant, or fools ; fair beauty's veil

Shrouds them in sun-like rays ; nought but the glory
    seen !

Beautiful I am : I know and hate it !

Beauty is valueless, unless it be

The handmaiden of love : and this we know,

Dwells not with us so fall'n.   It is reserv'd

For other realms : yet have spirits feelings,

And longings fierce : and though we cannot love,

We might be lov'd ; were we but visible

To mortal sight.

  SAT. And why not love ?

  SYL.   Love ! know you what you say ?

Were love in hell—'twould be no longer hell,

But Heaven !

I have a memory of what love was,

But now 'tis only torment to look back,

Upon that golden-rayed Orient,

From this abysm dark, where set our glory.

  SAT. Do I look back ? I, once high pinnacled

Above all bliss conceivable.   Of angels

Chief !   Nor forward !—no, despair is rest !

  SYL. Impossible is despair ; nor can we

Quench memory, until we cease to be.

My Hell is—love; yours—pride.   You hold a dream
Of empire.   Chief of fiends !   All that makes power
Of value, as honour, and truth and praise
Are ashes in your mouth.   Do we not know
That diamond throne, enfolding you around,
A quenchless fire ? your crown a diadem
Of lightning tined, piercing your tortur'd brain ?
That sceptre 'in your unconsumed hand,
Beneath which devils cower, is steel white hot ?
And I ! lost love the hell that burns me up ;
Lust of admiration—hate—jealousy,
And all the opposites of love.   For hearts !
Mine is a hollow, yours an iron heart,
Both glowing with unutterable pain !

 Sat. Then bear it : seek no change ; where hope
Can never enter.

 Syl.   I cannot : were I,
Even now, restored to my pristine state,
Sin, and the love of change would me ere long
Return to these nether realms.   Mortals say
That sin is its own punishment.   They lie ;
Men are not fools to peril all their hopes
Without a price,—and brave the penalty.
Sin is its own exceeding great reward,
Howe'er their casuists stultify themselves :
'Tis so to man ; but to us, immortal,

Sin is its own great punishment, because
We strive to intensify its pow'r—the source
Of all our sufferings, and cannot reap
Its fruit.   And yet I dare it, though I know
That tenfold woe will thence fall on my head.

SAT. Too well my spirit to your own responds
To fail your meaning : and from me you ask
For this, once giv'n, irrevocable gift,
To aid you to increase your sufferings.

SYL. Yes, Prince of Hell, give me but the power
Of being visible, I will repay
The boon, and bring a victim to your hate;
A noble one.

SAT.   Who is the mortal man
You would enslave? for 'tis not every one
That I have power to tempt.   Yet think again,
Before you plunge your sear'd heart in this fire.

SYL. Within the woodland shades wherein I dwell,
Where echo cadences my plaintive moans,
A youth I've seen—unseen—a prince of men ;
Listless and lone he wanders through the glades,
His bow unstrung, his quiver arrowless ;
Idly his hounds follow with heads down hung,
Regardless of the scarce alarmed herd,
Whose antlers glance among the distant trees ;
While leopards roam from Amanus, un-feared,

And drink at mid-day in Orontes' stream.

He feels he knows not what ; to me 'tis known ;

A female spirit 's more intuitive.

O, in a vacant heart what weakness lies !

Grant me my prayer ; I dare the suffering.

SAT. I know and hate him ; his nature 's noble,

But self-centred ; such I have pow'r to tempt :

Your prayer I grant.   Go, with seven-fold beauty,

And added grace on grace.   Be love his bane,

For he of love is capable.   How few

Of all the vaunted race of man, of whom

This were well said, a vile self-loving crew.

If pity for a man I e'er could feel,

Him would I pity in your venom'd toils.

Go forth ! prevail ! achieve his ruin !

Yours be the loss and mine the victory.

SYL. Yes ; all the boon within your pow'r to grant

Is added curse : therefore no thanks are due.

Away to the upper world !   [*Exit* SYLVIOLA.

SAT.   Say you so ?

You must be watch'd.   I doubt me you're within

The pale of the imprison'd ones to whom

Redemption is still offered.

Whispers a fiend who goes out.

Yes !   She speaks sooth : until we mem'ry quench,

Impossible is despair : yet, O Hell !

Barb'd by the certainty that no hope is.
Can I forget ? the thought still adds a pang
Of horror to my sum of anguish'd pain,
When the pure atmosphere of love no more
Could bear my frame up, weighted with its pride :
And I, as lightning fell ; fell down from heav'n ;
Fell as I stood—feet downward through the void ;
Mile upon mile I fell, both day and night,
Millions of miles I fell,—tearing my way
Through ether, cloud and storm ; my hair upborne
Rigid, by the upward rush of wind and hail :
My glorious wings stream'd after, powerless,
Guiding my arrowy fall.   Feet-down I fell !
Grasping the air, supportless, every nerve
Strain'd tight in torture by the shrinking soul ;
And the live thunder vengeful track'd my course ;
Sometime my horrent face and dilate eye
Turn'd heav'nward to the departing glory,
Evanishing from my accursed sight :
Then downward turned with abhorrent gaze
Into the dark, the bottomless descent,
Through which I, gasping, fell.

                    Downward I plung'd
Through ether, cloud and storm : the stars flew by,
And comets glar'd upon my hellward path ;
The moon increasing to my onward sight
Grew to a huge globe filling half the void ;

Then dwarf'd and dwindled to a silver shield,
As down I pass'd.   Millions of miles I fell !
The long, long pains of that tremendous fall
To anguish'd body, and constricted soul,
No tongue could tell.   Day after day I fell ;
And each moment held a madding horror
Summ'd up,—in a long age of suffering.
But worse—worse came ! when shuddering I clove
With skin exacerbate and breathless lung,
All agonis'd, the burning lake of Hell !
My shiv'ring form piercing the liquid fire,
Deep, deep, to its unfathomable depths,
So deep, that years seem'd to have pass'd and gone,
Ere my oppress'd and suffocated frame
Regain'd the upper air.   Can words describe
What agonies unspeakable I bore
In that incandescent abyss ?   My brain
Seeth'd in my charred skull ; boiling marrow
Scalded my aching bones ; my vitals wreath'd
With fervent flame ; my whole of sentient being
With magnified capacity for pain,
All burning with intolerable fire,
Yet undestroyed.
'Twas then the glorious panoply of wings
That shone around me—innocent—was lost,
And burnt up in that ocean of fierce fire,
Scorch'd to the bone and sinew : yet too soon

Replaced by these filthy batty vanes,

That wrap me coldly round, and darkly serve

To waft me through the regions of the damn'd.

Upheld by towering pride and stubborn will,

All, all the torments of the immortal frame

I sternly bore ; all :—but my riv'n soul

Had yet to bear a deep—more bitter wound ;

Impotent I bore it !—it rankles still ;—

O, fury ! oh, conscious madness ! worse than hell !

My soul had to endure the shame that He,

The One I had defied, should behold

My fall !　On earth He stood, incarnate God !

Triumphant stood, in human majesty,

And saw my fall.　Yes, He saw me fall !—me !

Me ! Lucifer ! as lightning fall from Heav'n,

And scath'd me with His pity !

And shall I not be aveng'd ? aveng'd upon

The god-like race of man He died to save,

And plunge them in equal ruin ?　And still

Will I—I hurl defiance 'gainst the throne

Of the Everliv—Ahh ! !

> *A crash of thunder : the lightning falls and hurls him*
> *from his throne ; and the scene closes amid awful*
> *reverberations, mingled with the terrific shrieks of*
> *the legions of fiends dying away into silence.*

———o———

SCENE 2.—*The Forest at Daphne. On one side an ancient hollow oak, with a gnarled doorway of natural Gothic, from which enter* SYLVIOLA.

SYL. O, what an ecstasy expands my being,
Now that I feel endued with a new power :
Man and fiend covet pow'r.   Beauty is pow'r,
And still is worshipp'd though her fanes are fall'n :
But this resplendent beauty that I bear
Would daze a mortal sight.   I must subdue
The demon fire within mine eyes that glows,
And then indue the robes of innocence,
Rob modesty of her veil, and heartless—borrow
The heart of sweetest sensibility,
And perfect woman seem.   Then will I weave
Around him my weird spell.   [*Exit through the trees.*

Enter CHRYSES.

CHRY. Whence this unease ? whence are these
   pained sighs ?
I feel as one cast forth on a hot waste,
Oppress'd with thirst—quenchless, unbearable :
I wander through these woods for rest, and list
The moanings of the wind among the trees,
And warbling of the waters as they flow,
And hear soft voices ton'd to my own woe.
Twice as I slept upon the emerald moss,

The velvet carpeting to these old oaks,
A vision rare I saw,—that almost spoke.
Without the sense how clear the spirit sees,
And hears and feels : this proves man immortal,
The body but the tools wherewith he works
In a material world.　This vision bright,
It could not be a dream, for the large eyes
Soft and dark,—full fill'd with glorious light,
Gaz'd into mine with a reality
Which sleep had baffl'd : nor when I awoke
Could I believe that it had pass'd away :
Certain I heard the rustle as of robes,
And light feet breaking 'mong the fall'n leaves.
What if I feign'd ?—O fool ! perchance renew
The fables of the fall'n goddesses,
Of whom some haunted erst these forest shades.
Yet I might feign,—though no divinity,
I doubt me something human will appear
To solve this mystery.　'Tis eventide ;
Here will I lie reclined, and hare-like watch
To realise this vision beautiful.

　　　　　　　He throws himself down as asleep, wild
　　　　　　　　　low music—then enter SYLVIOLA.

　　SYL. He sleeps, how peacefully he sleeps.　But
　　　hold !
This is no sleep.　The spirit I see not

Released by this temporary death—
The spirit hovering near its prostrate home,
Whose finer sense could see my essential form :
Perhaps I lose, by being visible,
This insight spiritual ; or perchance
His spirit's wafted upon mem'ry's wings
To scenes of other worlds, and mixes up,
As oft is seen, remembrances of things,
Events of years, in a short hour or two,
In such a madding dance confusing them,
The waking reason cannot catch its clue.

She approaches and gazes on him.

No, he sleeps not ; his bosom heaves, he moves.

CHRYSES *rises to his knee, speechless and immoveable, while she disappears.*

CHRY. Why am I spell-bound thus ? I could not speak ;
Even now my heart like a cag'd falcon
Dashes against its bars. I tremble—faint
With the strong rebound : and now she is gone !
O fool, to lose the opportunity !
Yet move I could not. Is this love ? is love
A reverential joy ? a worship wild ?
Its idol shrin'd in far off mystery ?
For this angel is a constellation
So high above my sphere, my soul despairs

To reach her glory's height : yet this I feel,
If she vouchsafe not to descend to me,
My soul will comet-like plunge onward forth
Into her realms of light, and die consum'd.
But where to seek her ?   Waking I saw her.
O hope arise ! not far can she be gone ;
These trees must have conceal'd her human form.
What though I scour the universal earth,
Search I must, and find my dream's reality.
Again my sense runs wild ; she is not far ;
And I will call and plead my loneliness,
And bend my voice to tones of tenderness ;
For women are as angels pitiful.
Lady ! saint ! angel ! by whatever name
I can adjure thee, hear my plaint ! O hear !
Appear and bless once more my desert sight
Blinded by sun-like rays.   O speak to me !
O let me hear the music which must flow
From so divine an instrument.   Appear !
For I have lost myself ; my wand'ring feet,
Among the mazes of these forest trees,
My soul in wilder mazes intricate.
Pity ! have pity on me—or I die !

           Enter SYLVIOLA *from the oak.*

   SYL. Who calls so piteously ? Ha ! I fear you !
   CHRY. 'Tis I should fear ! tell me—are you angel ?

SYL. How! what mean you? I am only woman.

CHRY. Only woman? O most perfect woman!
Clothed with every goddess' attribute,
I worship thee!

SYL.   You must not—this is wrong:
Worship is reserv'd for the immortals:
I am a simple maiden—you may love me.

CHRY. May I? This joy will kill me! O I will!
I do! I love you past all utterance!
And will you love me?

SYL.   No, I am less apt.
We like to be lov'd, but we do not love
Each wand'ring stranger that we meet withal;
And now I think on't, it is strange that I
Should venture this discourse with one unknown.
I came because you call'd; I thought, for help:
If you have lost your way I'll show it you;
And so farewell.

CHRY.   O do not banish me,
For dark will be my light, your presence gone.
O I will kneel to you, it is no crime:
O let me stay, and I will slave for you,
Be your servant—striving perchance to win
A smile in guerdon. O refuse me not.

SYL. What would you? 'Tis but a few minutes
    past

I knew you not—a stranger : now you ask—
I know not what you ask.

CHRY.   Only to be
Your servant—

SYL.   I should know whom I thus trust,
Perhaps some breaker of your country's laws,
Or bandit lurking 'gainst the traveller's peace.

CHRY. Has my deep love and worship deserv'd this ?
O it is you that have the pow'r to kill,
I but the pow'r to die !

SYL.   Well, you speak fair.

CHRY. My father is the ruler of this land ;
Where do you dwell ?

SYL.   O that is my secret.

CHRY. What fear you ?

SYL.   You might betray me.   O now
You look so pain'd I'll trust you ; your promise
I would not trust : words and protestations
Are so much breath—clouds to envelope guile :
But to the true heart that looks forth wordless
From the open face—to this would I trust
My life.   Now follow.

*They enter the oak. Scene changes to a furnished room,
with Gothic windows, veiled by vines and flowering
plants.*

SYL. Welcome ! how like you this—my fairy hall ?

CHRY. A sweet retreat : with you to lighten it,
A paradise !

SYL. O if you flatter, I withdraw my trust.

CHRY. Flattery I hate ; but may I not praise?
I cannot flatter you.

SYL.   O worse and worse,
These common arts meseems you've practised
On many poor maids' hearts, deceiving them ;
Where did you learn this lore ?

CHRY.   Most beautiful!
Of art or practice I am innocent,
The only master that has taught me, love.
But tell me your dear name, and I will bind
And couple with it in my mind all thoughts
Of beauty, worth and grace ; and when praise-full
I utter it, you will not say I flatter.

SYL. O fraudful scholar of deceiving love,
My name I'll give ycu, lest you should exhaust
All epithets, and fall to repetition.
I'm call'd Sylviola.

CHRY.   Sylviola ! Sylviola!
How sweet it falls in music from your lips
To mine, making mine musical ;
Harsh names beauty can beautify,
But this is tun'd to every harmony :
Strike but one string of the melodious lyre,

The others vibrate in true unison ;
So when this name I name, upon my mind
Will rise all forms of beauty, grace and joy ;
And when I want a name to comprehend
All perfect loveliness, I'll say—Sylviola !
Sylviola ! O seraph azure-eyed !
Sit there array'd in queen-like majesty,
While I a suppliant at your feet implore
Some service to perform for your lov'd sake,
And crown my loyalty.

SYL.   And yet I doubt
That, should the time come charg'd with any peril,
Your loyalty would not abide the proof.

CHRY. But that I am so happy by your side,
And would not tempt a kindly Providence,
I could have wished that nations had been leagued,
And mountains pil'd, to sever me from you ;
Or that you would some daring task appoint
Within earth's confines, e'en to the verge of hell ;
A power I feel to raze all obstacles,
O'er all triumphant when inspired by you.

SYL. O talk of possibilities, not dreams ;
'Tis easier far to o'ercome an outward foe,
Than unwind prejudice coil'd round the heart,
Or conquer self.   So the banner'd hero
That all unequal arm'd would dare the fight,
And lead his thousands 'gainst a serried million,

In peace is slave to some base appetite,
Or vanquish'd by a whim conventional.

   CHRY. What mean you?

   SYL.   You are of a noble house,
Say that I were a low-born peasant child—

   CHRY. Say the sun were the fire of a smithy,
This is a pure impossibility,
Although your mother swore, not credible;
Her falsing tongue could not my true eyes blind
To the perfection that would gild a crown.

   SYL. I said suppose—and now I'll put the case—
I were a slave: Oh then a golden show'r
Would be the form your market-love would take,
My humble will not ask'd.

   CHRY.   Oh! now you jest:
But pain me not with playful blasphemy
Against the queen of my idolatry.

   SYL. (*aside*) And must I lure such true love to
      perdition?
I feel—I feel a glimmering of good—
That prompts to pity: I am not—all lost.

             The FIEND *rises.*

   FIEND. Beware!

   SYL. Ha! protect me!

               As she sinks, CHRYSES *supports her in*
                   his arms. FIEND *disappears.*

   CHRY. You faint, Sylviola; why this shudder?

And now I look on your dear face I see
Fell horror mar its beauty.   How is this?

SYL. Ask not,—'twill pass,—it has already pass'd:
Do I look better now?

CHRY.   So beautiful!

SYL. What was I saying?   O, to set you tasks;
If I required test of your boasted love
That you some deed of baseness should enact.

CHRY. What?

SYL. Did I not know he would refuse me?
Betray your friend, or slay mine enemy
In the dark.

CHRY.   I!

SYL.   Poor love 'gainst prejudice!
Or raise some dire sedition in the state,
Do sacrilege :——

CHRY.   Enough, Sylviola.
Though hell-born fancies flow from angel lips
They can no more the crystal spirit stain,
Than poison poured from a purple vase
Of amethyst affect its purity.
Nothing but good can emanate from you.

SYL. You cannot know my heart; you still evade,
And answer not to any case I ask.
All are to evil prone, then why not I?
Answer to my demand.

CHRY.   I would do it—

I would do all you ask ; 'tis easy said,

For well I know if it were possible

That you should ask, 'twould be no longer you.

SYL. A simple girl, I can no further track

Your wily speech.   But now you must leave me,

Already have you stay'd too long.

CHRY.   Too long ?

I thought it but a moment : I obey :

When may I come again ?

SYL.   Why come again ?

Well, the forest's free to all ; to-morrow

If you happen on the hour of the twelve

When I walk forth, at eve you'll see me there.

CHRY. When will the leaden wings of time o'erpass

The interval ?   How will existence drag

Through all the weary hours until that time ?

SYL. Farewell !

CHRY. Till then, farewell Sylviola.   [*Exeunt.*

——o——

SCENE 3.—*The Forest.* SYLVIOLA *on a mossy seat.* *Enter*
     CHRYSES, *and kneels to her.*

CHRY. Once more at your dear feet Sylviola,

Forgotten the dark ages that have pass'd

Since yesterday, O happiness ! O joy !

K

SYL. No, happiness exists not; and your joy
Will be as transient as all other joys.

CHRY. Yes, alas, as transient as your presence:
No more; but that too much — for you will go,
And with you heaven and all my happiness.
But why do you speak thus?

SYL.   O I have fears:
With tests of faith I tried you yesterday,
To which you would not answer, but did glance
Beside the purpose: yet how far 'bove all
Is the great sacrifice I ask from you:
For love is—self-sacrifice—or nothing.

CHRY. Is't my life?

SYL.   No, far more: when you know all
You will not love me.

CHRY. Oh! and do you care?

SYL. Perhaps I do, I have no other friend.

CHRY. O with this trancing hope, Sylviola,
Of love return'd, what is the sacrifice
I am not equal to?

SYL.   How shall I speak?

CHRY. You do not trust my love.

SYL. Ah, beware!

CHRY.   O speak!

SYL. You will repent your importunity.

CHRY. O, I can find it in my heart to die
For you; to give up father, brother, all;
Break every tie that binds me to my kind:
What is there you can ask and I refuse?

SYL. Between us two exists a barrier
Of which you dream not.

CHRY.   How! what can there be?

SYL. Then hear: I do not serve your God. You
   pale!

CHRY. Ha! say you sooth?

SYL.   And so I've lost your love!

CHRY. Horror has blanched my cheek, Sylviola!
You—you an infidel!

SYL.   Yet I love you!

CHRY. O crush me not between these opposites:
You say you love me! With one hand you pour
Into my soul an ecstacy of joy,
With the other—misery and despair:
Yet, if you love me, I can brave the worst.

SYL. So dearly O my Chryses! but why thus?
Why this transport? there is no difference;
Jehovah, Jove, or whatsoe'er men call
Their god, he is still the same god to all;
Were yours the god alone, would half the world
Be left in ignorance of him? You serve
The queen of heaven and fall down before

A virgin whimpled in a silken stole :
I worship—beauty incarnate,—Ashtaroth,
Whom you altho' you deem it not obey,
While yet ungrateful.

  CHRY.   Lost ! so lost ! And I ?

 SYL. Beloved, have I not said—I love you ;
And for my love, alas ! too easy given—

 CHRY. Sylviola, have pity on me ! else
Will madness sear my brain : as the martyr
With loving eyes looks up when the fierce flames
Enwrap his limbs, so does my love triumph
Over my anguish'd spirit when I look
On you.

    The FIEND *rises invisible.*

 SYL. O we will make a heav'n of our own —
A heav'n of love. I do not ask your life,
Or mountains to remove ; but this strange faith
To cast aside, a garment threadbare worn,
A superstition made up by the wise
To rule the mob of fools : you are above
Being gyved by such trammels. It is not much
I ask for all my love.

  CHRY.   Sylviola !
My beautiful ! my bride ! I am all yours ;
And I will sacrifice my life, my faith,
All, all for you !

SYL.   My own, my Chryses!
Now do I know you love me, when for me
You will forsake your God.

CHRY.   Ha! said I so?
Forsake my God?   What though I said I did,
The lip's breath cannot change the fixed soul :
What tho' I denied Him, my heart would still
Be filled with his love, and mock my tongue ;
Say, that I took an oath to you that I
Believed not; still should I swear by Him,
The living God, and contradict my oath.
It were far easier to put off myself,
Than separate me from the life of Him
Who died for me.   But you Sylviola,
Why will you not believe on Him and live?
O by the love you say you bear to me!
O by the deep love that I seal with this !

He kisses her.

As we are one, so be we one in faith.

   SYL. (*aside*) Ha! that kiss! like a bright wave it
      courses
Through my veins, and breaks love crested 'gainst my
      heart—
That dark fane of hate, can love enter there?
Yes, I love him—I that would destroy him :
He conquers me.

The Fiend *appears.   The* Angel *descends.*

Fiend. Once more, beware !

Ang. Spirit, fear not :

For greater far is He that is for you,

Than he that is against you. *They disappear.*

Chry. Sylviola ! my own ! Sylviola !

Why stand you thus amaz'd ? what look you on ?

The hands I kiss are cold, and your eyes blaze

With fire unnatural : what do you see ?

Syl. What you—can—not.   O let me lay my head

Upon your breast, and hear your human heart

Sobbing with loving sympathy ; there rest

While yet it may, though anguish harrows mine.

Chry. Lie there for ever, O my beautiful !

Would my own heart were wrung with suffering,

Could it but free thine from a single pang !

What dost thou fear ?   No harm shall come to thee ;

Hover they yet the gods that you have served,

In dread imagination o'er your head ?

No gods are they who come in horrent forms

Of fear : there is one only God, whose name

Is love.   He can protect—

Syl.   O I feel it ;

I feel my nature changed.   Cast me not off

In this my misery.   Not for myself,

My soul is full of a great grief for you,

For you I've lured to a fatal love,

Dread,—hopeless,—never to be realised!

The FIEND *appears.*

Hear me, Chryses, hear me : you love—fiends hence !—

FIEND *disappears.*

Love makes me free—I am—

CHRY. Oh, what?

SYL. A spirit!

CHRYSES *falls senseless to the earth.*

She takes him in her arms.

Wake! O beloved! wake! Now to my soul
Bursts in, as water rushing o'er its bounds,
Love in its power : my arid soul absorbs,
As a dry desert burnt, the torrent vast
That floods it ! Awake, my beloved, wake!
I clasp him to my heart and kiss his lips,
As tho' I'd drain the little life remains ;
This horror killed him. Wilt thou not revive?
Save him, ye gods ! Ye cannot save yourselves.
Triumph, ye fiends ! Yet no, he is not yours.
His pale cheek on my breast, within mine arms he lies,
A sculptur'd angel. O have I slain him ?
No, his heart beats—a sigh—let love's kisses
Wake thee to life. Ope thine eyes and bless me.

CHRY. (*reviving*) Am I in heaven, Sylviola ? if not,
To die, to go there from such happiness,
'Twill be no difference. Love makes both one.

SYL. O transient joy ! yet I hold you—love you !

CHRY. You said,—now I remember,—that you were
An angel.

SYL.   O no, but as far beyond
The reach of human love.

CHRY.   Sylviola!
All true love is divine ; it has no bounds
Of body, feature, form ; of life or death ;
But once enkindled at the heav'nly fount,
Space cannot bound it and it fills all time
Here and beyond.   When suddenly you said
That you were not of this world, the strange blow
Stagger'd my human nature, ever weak
And shrinking from the supernatural :
Now my soul rises to its throne immortal,
And shakes off the bondage of humanity :
Spirit to spirit—I can love you still ;
And when deliver'd from this fleshly shrine,
My soul will find yours in the realms of light,
And love be perfected, ineffable in bliss.

SYL. O what a love is this ! 'tis love divine.
Your life a ruin, yet you love me still :
Beyond all thought is such self-sacrifice.

CHRY. The earth of love I sacrifice to gain
The empyrean ; where love never wanes,
But stay, the glorious vision fades : O grief !
What is the sacrifice of earthly love

To loss eternal? the vacant future?

You said—you said—you served earthly gods.

SYL. No, love has freed me from th' infernal band :

No longer do I serve them.

The FIEND appears.

CHRY. O joy!—but yet you do not worship mine.

And if to die for my own happiness

You call a sacrifice,—conceive,—O think

Of that great love——

FIEND.   Away, and hear no more.

CHRY. Why smile in scorn?

SYL.   Not at your words : go on.

CHRY. Of that great love transcending human thought,

That died for us alone, His enemies !

O magnanimity !

O love, pure, unalloyed ! astonishment

Of angels wondering ! confounding hell !

Could you have heard His words, or seen as I

With the mind's eye His glory.

SYL.   Listen : I have.

FIEND. Dar'st thou rebel?   He advances on her.

SYL.   Ah ! good angels guard me !

The ANGEL appears.

ANG. Depart ! nor with unhallow'd step profane,

Unholy one, this sacred place. Depart !

FIEND. I must obey ; I quail before his glance ;

Let Satan come himself and cope with him
An if he dare ; for me my task is done.

                         The FIEND *disappears.*

     CHRY. What moves you thus, Sylviola ?

     SYL.   'Tis past :

Yes ! I have seen him. It was on that day
When through the city's breadth was heard the cry
Of triumph from The sacrificing Christ,
" It is finish'd ! " All earth gave back the cry,
And Hades echoed through its vast expanse
Of convoluted cave and rock-dom'd hall,
" It is finish'd ! " Then trembled the Arch-Fiend,
And from his throne fled to the lowest hell
With all his angels, comates of his pride ;
And we were left, trembling, a spirit band
By sin seduced, although we had not join'd
His proud rebellion 'gainst the Holy One ;
In a vast hall we stood—sunless and dim ;
Earth's granite pillars centre-bas'd upheld
The awful dome, floor of the living world ;
Dark was the light as when the sun forsakes
The northern pole : myriads of spirits
Here stood, or knelt, or flew ; a wondrous throng :
In groups they stood or hung in wreaths around,
But gain'd no courage from companionship.
Sudden a glory fillèd all the space

And all the scene was light; amid the dark
And flowing stoles the pale, white faces gleam'd
Like stars upon the galaxy at night;
Most beautiful they were, but on each face
Was horror limn'd and terror and despair;
And the light passed on through all the length
And breadth of the vast hall, and lighted up
Its most concealèd shades, till every soul
Living within the hall stood in that light,
And the light passed on; where stalactite
And crystal pillar hung of crysolite,
Emerald and gem; where pendant column hung
Age-filter'd from the crust of upper earth,
And petrified within this nether world;
Enormous, overhead, but seldom seen,
Or imag'd in the gloom; now lighted up
They blazed and rejoic'd with a new joy,
Flickering, sparkling, casting all around
Myriad reflexions from their colour'd prisms,
In rays of flashing light across the dome;
Then wound and crossed and pour'd their refract light
In gold and diamond through the gorgeous hall
Illuminate!
All veil'd their faces.   When we look'd again,
A Presence stood before us; of a form
Magnificent in beauty glorious,

Of a face—all love.   Love shone upon his brow,
And from his eyes beam'd love—while from
His lips mellifluous flow'd a living stream of love ;
Then lovingly he warn'd us to repent,
While yet the long-suffering of His Father stay'd,
With words of such persuasive pow'r, each word
Moved the heart as though it had been a tear.
And then I heard a sound of weeping low,
And from ten thousand hearts throughout the throng
Unnumbered—a mournful sobbing rose,
Cadenc'd away to the remotest bounds
Of the unfinite void.   And then I turn'd,
And far and near were sorrowing faces fixed
In silent adoration on their God ;
And as contrition stole into their souls,
Vanish'd all terror from their looks—cast out
By perfect love ; while on their features shone
Reflected glory from the Holy One,
Enorbing them, and all their robes were white !
Again that loving voice, " Come unto Me,
O come all ye that are athirst and take
Freely the water of eternal life."
And then there follow'd Him a shining band,
Irradiate, and casting wavering light
On the sad faces that were left behind.
So the light wan'd from out the dome and hall,
  Gilding each jutting rock and pendent spire ;

A moment glanc'd on crystal point and gem,
A moment gleam'd upon despairing eyes :
Then the band passed forth : and all was dark !

CHRY. O wonderful ! and you—Sylviola?

SYL. Alas, no tear from my hard heart distill'd
To cool my burning eye : and I went back
To feel the hourly, daily, yearly strain
Of self-inflicted, anguish'd hopelessness,
Like unto madness knowing oneself mad.
But did I hear unmov'd the Holy One
In all the power of his eloquence,
Now to be chang'd by you ?

CHRY.   It is not I.
O no—it is His voice that speaks in me :
Think that you hear again His glorious word,
Think that you see again that face of love
Whose image on your soften'd heart has borne
Remembrance of Him down the lapse of time.
Sylviola, He died for you.

SYL. Love conquers hate !   God's love and thine :
O love omnipotent !   Forgive, forgive !
All other gods I utterly abjure
And trust in only Him—the One Redeemer !

Enter SATAN.

Lo ! the Arch-Fiend appears !   Save, O save me !

She rushes into the arms of CHRYSES.

The ANGEL *interposes.*

SATAN. Why dost thou stay me from mine own?
   the child

Of Hell?   I want not the mortal victim.

ANG. Redeemed both !   May The Lord rebuke thee,
O Satan ! even The Lord rebuke thee.

Is not this a brand out of the fire pluck'd ?

> AZRAEL *descends as a glorious Angel, veiled,*
>   *with a bright star above his forehead.*

AZRAEL. Come away ye blessed ones !   I'm sent for
   you.

CHRY. O now I see eternity unclose

Its glorious gates ! O rapture—ecstasy !

Come Sylviola—fair spirit, come.   On,

Lead on, bright messenger !

SYL.   I come, O joy !

O bliss ineffable ! O triumphant love !

Sav'd ! sav'd !   AZRAEL *leads them up.*

SATAN. Lost ! lost ! both slave and victim :   still
   vanquish'd !

ANG. Descend, rebellious one ! and know that Love
Is stronger far than Hate, than Death,

And all the powers of Hell.   To thine own place

Descend ! descend !

> *Exit,* SATAN *retreating, charioted by dark*
>   *clouds, and disappearing against the red*
>   *glow of the setting sun.   Solemn music.*

VISIONS OF EARTH.

Lo, all is nought but flying vanity !
So I that know this world's inconstancies,
Sith only God surmounts all times decay,
In God alone my confidence do stay.

SPENSER.

KOORDISTAN.

I.

I passed through a region earthquake torn,
And saw a glorious rainbow's colour'd sheen;
One foot upon a rushing river borne,
The other on a distant sunlit scene;
While black as night the mountain and the storm
Darkly behind it rose, brightning its crescent form.

II.

This vision shone with ev'ry jewel's hue,
The golden topaz, and the em'rald green,
The crimson ruby, and the sapphire blue,
With orange deep, and violet pale between;
Blending in loving harmony so true,
That each the other did with its own tincts imbue.

III.

Embracing with broad arms this gorgeous bow,
I saw another stand in fainter dyes;
Her partner's beauties with responsive glow,
Sweetly she blushed forth in modest guise;
So did her image from the other flow,
Like as a maiden fair in a bright glass doth shew.

IV.

And when the one did fade the other pal'd ;
And when this brighten'd that again was fair ;
The fair one vanish'd if the bright one fail'd ;
Whether in storm or shine a linked pair :
This beauteous sight no sooner had I hail'd,
Than I with grief of heart their ruin sad bewail'd.

V.

For now the veil wherein their forms were shrin'd
By the sharp lightning's edge was rudely rent ;
And the black frowning clouds with thunder lin'd
From lowering wreaths the vollied echoes sent ;
Their frail shapes trembling on the rising wind,
One hesitates to go and leave its mate behind.

VI.

But soon the storm from heav'n sweeps amain ;
The crags, the woods, the river and the vale,
Are hidden by its vast funereal train :
Then from the dying bows their colours fail,
And all their glories from the earth do wane ;
While the bereaved skies fall weeping all in rain.

PERSIA.

I.

I saw two doves clothed with golden wings,
Coral their feet, their eyes were ruby red,
Each swelling neck a pearled collar rings,
And lustrous light their changing plumes o'erspread,
Gracefully their waving necks entwining ;
All other doves in beauty far outshining.

II.

Basking they sat upon a bared branch,
Now cooing lovingly, now murmuring low ;
Of no ill dreaming fate 'gainst them can launch ;
Billing closely with undulating flow ;
Rising, falling, with beguiling motion ;
So the lucid shell floats on the silent ocean.

III.

Then side by side they slept, this happy pair ;
Their voices sank into a whisper sweet ;
The leaves sigh'd round them, and the balmy air
Lull'd them to rest while still their hours did fleet ;
Their breasts against the smooth bough pressed were,
And with their feathers fair cover'd their coral feet.

IV.

I saw an eagle wheel his spiral flight,
Circling cloudward still he wheeled higher :
I heard his shrill scream, while the sunny light
Shone through his barrèd wings like feather'd fire ;
Still higher soaring in the effulgent height,
I heard his clarion cry though lost to mortal sight.

V.

A shadow passes sudden 'cross the sun ;
Upwards I gaze, and in the highest sky
A little speck at first I see it come ;
Larger and larger yet it cometh nigh ;
With meteor swoop and bright eye flashing doom,
Downward it cometh fleet rushing on rapid plume.

VI.

The bough was vacant when I look'd again,
Whereon those loving doves had gone to rest ;
I saw the eagle upward gently plane,
Bearing their mangled beauties to his nest ;
Their happy loves exchanged for dying pains,
As slowly to the sky he sail'd on silent vanes.

MOROCCO.

I.

Slowly floating down an Eastern river,
I came to where a goodly garden grew;
Green its foliage seem'd to have been ever,
So fast the trees their fallen leaves renew:
I moor'd my boat and landed in the shade
Of leafy woven boughs a canopy that made.

II.

The citron cast its fragrance on the air,
Strewing its bridal blossoms all around;
The pomegranate its blushing flowers there
Commingling with them, beautified the ground;
The little flowers that grew among the grass
Faint and oppressed lie under the perfum'd mass.

III.

The festoon'd grapes in sculptured clusters hung,
And juicy apricot with golden skin ;
From its broad flags the golden melon sprung,
And purple mulberries the leaves between ;
Blue figs and other fruits I did not miss,
Nor veiled peach that blushes from the sun's warm kiss.

IV.

Deep in this garden's most secluded nook
I found an arbour form'd for cool repose ;
And by it curl'd a lucent warbling brook
O'er pebbles rough that sweetly singing goes ;
The night bird fill'd the garden with its song,
Where screen'd from heat it sits the darkling shades
    among.

V.

The red rose hung above me, intertwin'd
With scented jessamine and moon-flow'rs white—
Whose blossoms through the dark green foliage wind
With peeping eyes, like stars upon the night ;
And berries bright strung upon curling bines,
And lovely trailing plants veiling the grot with vines.

VI.

I heard a strange sound as of rushing hail,
Nathless the air was clear, no cloud above,
Nearer it came with a mysterious wail,
And then a rustling as of wings that move ;
And then I saw with fell destruction tined
The fatal locust army coming down the wind.

VII.

Onwards it moved in measureless array,
The front ranks swarm'd the earth, while o'er them
     flew
Successive swarms, a glittering display
Of wings as smoke, bringing destruction new ;
Like prairie fire driven by the wind,
Before them all is green, and all is black behind.

VIII.

The river stops them not ; some fly, some swim ;
Myriads are drowned, yet still the columns pass
Stretching their serried ranks from rim to rim ;
The bank o'erleaping, sullying all the grass,
They climb the hedge all wasting in their track ;
And now this garden fair with famine fresh attack.

IX.

Before the coming doom each flower pales,
And shudder all the trees that garden through
As climbs the van and leaf and fruit assails ;
While the hind ranks their onward march renew ;
Ruthless o'er all the living torrent flows,
And o'er their beauty lost the south wind sobbing blows.

X.

The trees lift up their bare arms to the sky,
The arbour shows a ragged tangled mass ;
The winter's tooth could not have " bit so nigh,"
The drought would spare some flowret in the grass :
This fell scourge pass'd with fruit and flowers' breath,
Leaving to mark its course but blackness—ashes—
    death !

XI.

Ah ! woe is me, for this fair garden's pride,
All whelmed in ruin in one little hour :
Who tell of this world's happiness have lied,
When so dark storm so suddenly could lour ;
And scene so fair of trancing loveliness
Vanish, and leave nought but memory of its bliss.

BARBARY.

I.

I saw a horse full stately pace the plain,
White was his hue as newly fall'n snow,
And white his mane and sweeping volum'd train ;
His eyes and nostrils with red flames did glow ;
Black were his legs, and his round hocks did look,
Mottl'd with moony spots, like pebbles in the brook.

II.

High is his crest, his foot disdains the ground,
The foam flies from his bit, his flashing eye,
Glancing from side to side on all around,
Courts admiration as he passes by ;
No motion can deceive his vivid sight,
Nor sound of danger 'scape his ear in darkest night.

III.

His curtain'd mane falls waving to his knee
In rippling radiance as he walks along,
To roll in thunder when with madding glee
He charges through death's hail the foes among ;
But now in gentlest majesty he stands
Wrinkling his velvet mouth soft as a lady's hands.

IV.

Of vermeil silk was his caparison,
Embroider'd round with golden flowers brave ;
With gold and silver bit and stirrup shone,
And tassell'd fringes round about him wave,
While from beneath hangs down a leopard's spoil,
Cinque spotted on a ground of yellow foil.

V.

I saw, until upon a foray went
This gentle steed his master's will obeying ;
Until from hurtling shot, with banner rent,
His unmatch'd fleetness sav'd his lord from slaying :
But, lo, a little spot upon his side,
That as he rushed past with fatal stain was dyed.

VI.

Soon, failing fast, he fell in mortal pain ;
Over his white skin stream'd his crimson blood ;
With mute appeal his dying eyes complain :
His master savèd sad beside him stood ;
Till dead, his trappings marr'd by life's dark stain
He took, and sorrowing left him on the plain.

VII.

Scarce had he fallen, when streaming one by one
From the clear vault where they had watch'd unseen,
The vultures from the four winds flocking come,
Like evil angels from hell's realms I ween ;
In mantling plumes round throng these obscene things ;
I marvell'd so ill birds possess'd such glorious wings.

VIII.

This beauteous creature, lo, become the prey
Of felon birds ! they tear his glossy hide,
They gorge his flesh, his comeliness bewray,
And of his glories sully all the pride :
Thus all that's beautiful must come to spoil,
Vain is the glory born, alas, on earthly soil.

ENGLAND.

I.

A vision rises of my own dear land,
A crystal stream winding thro' pleasant meads,
With drooping pensive cowslips all o'ergemm'd,
And cuckoo flow'rs and other lovely weeds ;
Nestling in mossy banks the sweet primrose,
Fairest of wild flowers upon the earth that grows.

II.

A hazel copse here juts into the stream,
Dropping its brown nuts with a bell-like tone ;
There, through an oak-crown'd hill the sun-rays beam
Upon a yellow cliff around whose zone
Th' impatient waters flash and dance and swirl ;
Then sweep to th' other bank in many a dimpling whirl.

III.

The evanescent May flies rise and fall,
In cadenc'd music to the rippling river,
Sunning their gauzy wings ; to be soon, all
Whelmed in the fickle flood for ever ;
Like human joys one little hour that blaze,
Perish, and leave the heart in sorrowful amaze.

IV.

On either side the green woods now close in,
The stream sleeps calmly in a placid pool ;
And in this pool a noble trout doth swim,
Joyous disporting in the waters cool :
The little trouts that round about him sport,
The glitt'ring courtiers seem about a prince's court.

V.

Sometimes he glances like a beam of light,
Sometimes as waving water weed, lies still ;
Now from the surface smooth a shower bright
Of diamond drops into the air doth spill ;
Then warily he glides beneath the beds
Of water-cresses wreath'd that toss their plumy heads.

VI.

I saw a gilt and gaudy colour'd fly,
Wherein was hid a little barb of steel,
Upon the water lighting merrily ;
Deceit can paint the false in semblance real ;
This beauteous fish updarting with a spring
The garish fraud to seize, fled struck by mortal sting.

VII.

In vain he dives into the pool's dark caves
To free himself against the gnarled roots ;
Or mid the tangl'd weedy masses laves,
Or with strong spine the foaming rapid shoots ;
All struggles vain : the fisher's landed prize,
Helpless upon the grass he palpitating lies.

VIII.

His silver scales all dropped with ruby gems,
His back bespotted like the ounce's hide,
His red gills pant, quiver his scarlet fins
Wherewith he wont upon the waters ride ;
Resplendent colours flicker'd o'er his side ;
I watch'd the changing tints until he slowly died.

IX.

Thus to death betray'd was this fair creature,
Like man among the vain world's mazes stray'd,
His heart still set on all that's bright in feature,
To be the dupe of gauds in truth array'd,
Unless High God, Who sees all latent guile,
Quench each deadly shaft in the glory of His smile.

DREAMLAND.

I.

What saw I in my dreaming consciousness !
Was it a fading vision from the skies?
Or wingless seraph 'scaped from heav'nliness?
No 'twas a maiden sweet with glorious eyes,
Such eyes as men imagine angels given,
So deep so blue so pure, lit from the fount of heaven.

II.

How to describe this maiden's comeliness
Is not within the power of my quill ;
And with black ink to paint fair, were amiss,
And with unskilful lines my page to fill :
Yet must I strive her beauty to rehearse,
Or lose before the end the moral of my verse.

III.

Her parted hair first caught heav'n's light and glow'd,
Then rippled waving to her bosom white ;
Smooth swerving thence to her lithe waist it flow'd,
And down her shoulders roll'd a torrent bright ;
Her fair white skin shines through the twined hairs,
As through a waterfall a marble rock appears.

IV.

The living colour on her cheek that lies,
Softens away by beauty's own hand blanch'd ;
The velvet arches 'bove her starry eyes
Are bows through which are glancing arrows launch'd ;
Wild innocence hath limn'd the features of her face
With gentleness and joy and every virgin grace.

V.

Could I embody music, or the hues
Of sunset, or the breezes of the south,
From ever changing form and colour choose,
Perchance I might describe her beauteous mouth ;
And yet the trancing smile that round it plays,
Still would unfix'd remain a glorious maze.

VI.

She gather'd up the bright waves of her hair,
And wove them in a twisted coronal
Around her lovely head and temples fair ;
Still down her neck some heavy tresses fall ;
Then pensively upon her arm reclin'd,
While in her radiant face shone forth the living mind.

VII.

I saw a flying dove on pinions fleet
Chas'd by a falcon fierce from out the sky ;
I saw it fall exhausted at her feet
With drooping wing and soft imploring eye ;
With pity mov'd she raised it from the ground,
The while the baffled hawk soar'd up and wheel'd around.

VIII.

In her warm bosom laid as in a nest,
She still'd its panting heart with sweet caress
And smooth'd its golden wings and sunlit breast,
Soothing its fears with low-toned tenderness :
Murmuring, with kissing bill, the gentle dove
As with a human voice return'd her lavish'd love.

M

IX.

And then she slept upon a blossom'd bank,
With violets o'erspread and pansies pyed ;
All round about her tall flowers strove in rank
With blushing screen her loveliness to hide ;
Shadow'd the flow'rs their tracery o'er her side,
And with their vermeil tincts her ivory skin was dyed.

X.

But now I saw a wonder in my dream ;
This guileful dove its feathers 'gan to change,
And scales and linked chains of gilded gleam
In long enamelled pattern to arrange ;
The flatt'ning head a serpent form did take ;
Lo ! in her bosom warm lay coiled a chilly snake !

XI.

Unwinding slow his undulating neck,
He waver'd round her hair and eyes and lips ;
(His life late sav'd, ah, little did he reck ;)
Awhile his quivering tongue the honey sips,
Then rear'd with glittering eye his scaly crest,
And struck his deadly fangs into her velvet breast.

XII.

She felt it not, but soon the poison slow
Through the blue veins too swiftly cours'd its way,
And by degrees her heart-blood ceas'd to flow,
And her bright form as pallid marble lay.
With sudden start and with suppressed scream
Trembling and sad I woke.—'Twas,—and 'twas not a
    dream !

XIII.

Alas, why is all love alloyed with hate ?
Why is this world the theatre of wrong ?
Why is all beauty made the snare of fate ?
The noblest why the victim of the strong ?
And innocence in all its loveliness
Ever the prey of guile and subtle craftiness ?

OCEAN.

I.

Like to a glorious swan array'd in white,
I saw a gallant ship put out to sea ;
Her pennons flutter, and her ensign bright
Flames on the breeze—a noble Argosy !
Her bosom'd prow the dark green water laves,
Proudly she moveth on amid the rippling waves.

II.

Her tall masts tower into the far blue,
Her sails spread out unwrinkled to the wind,
Her yards the thoughts of Zion's Cross renew,
And love of God for all of human kind.
With stay and cord tense as a harper's strings,
Onward she passeth forth like a bright thing with wings.

III.

Parting the crescent waves with eager prow,
Exultingly she gains the open main ;
The winds laugh round her and the sunbeams glow,
The sunlight glows and the winds laugh again ;
Caressingly the waves her bosom kiss,
Then pass away foam-crested with a seething hiss.

IV.

But now the winds and waves have ceas'd their play,
The winds howl wildly o'er the heaving waste,
The waves arise and hurl their torrent spray,
The sun is hid, the sky by dark clouds laced ;
Fast the brave ship, battling their mingled ire,
Flies through the troubled sea cresting the waves with
    fire.

V.

Then one by one the sails are gather'd in,
And her gaunt masts half naked lash the clouds ;
Soon their aspiring tops are lower'd in :
Strong blows the pain'd gale through the straining
    shrouds,
And lacerates itself and fiercely shrieks ;
Then weeps a stormy rain, torn by red levin streaks.

VI.

The little sail that she can show on high,
All torn and rent streams far on the black storm,
All conquering the gale careers the sky,
Down fall the masts leaving the ship forlorn ;
Under the cruel surge she helpless reels,
And with a human heart her threatened doom she feels.

VII.

Full low upon her side she now doth lie,
The traitor waves o'erwhelm the doomed hull
With glassy sheets that over her fast fly,
All aided by the wind with fury full :
Than hatred wreaked on mere enemies,
The love all turned to hate, alas, more bitter is.

VIII.

And now she leaks from every open seam,
And struggles vainly 'gainst her coming fate ;
The thunders rock the sky, the lightnings gleam,
The faithless elements exhaust their hate :
She shudders—sinks—the wild winds madly rave ;
And the hoarse waves roar out triumphing o'er her
grave.

IX.

And thou art gone in all thy beauty's pride,
No more to be the sport of hopes and fears :
Thus man trusts still life's fickle wind and tide,
Knowing full well their bitter fruit is tears.
Thus youth floats beautiful on love's fair sea ;
Betrayal,—ruin,—death,—all braving recklessly.

WOODLAND.

I.

I wandered through a park among the trees,
Winding my way through heath and tangled fern,
And pass'd a lakelet rippled by the breeze,
From whose green sedge arose a lonely hern
Trailing his dripping legs with bended throat,
That as he sailed away gave forth a mournful note.

II.

Until I came to a sweet grassy glade,
In midst of which a noble oak did grow ;
Its gnarled trunk was like a tower made,
And its broad arms spread far around and low ;
Through foliage dark a net of boughs it weaves,
While crowns its glorious head a century of leaves.

III.

Where cast the roofed boughs a shadow deep,
And drop their acorns from a thousand cups,
At highest noon the antler'd deer do sleep,
And the red butterfly the leaf dew sups.
Hark! warblings wild from its green depths are heard,
Where hid in verdure thick sings each sweet throated bird.

IV.

The merle with orange bill and mourning plume,
And song-thrush brown with spotted bosom white,
And dear lov'd robin with his breast of bloom,
And nightingale the mother of delight,*
And whitethroat shy tuning his under lay,
While railing in despite forth flashes the blue jay.

V.

Oft have I listened in its shade reclin'd
To all its utterances; from whispers low
Creeping through all its leaves, to moanings blind,
When through its heart the bitter breezes blow,
And the deep bass that from its centre calls,
As strains the roaring storm, and cracks its russet walls.

VI.

A hundred times hast thou thy leaves renew'd,
Still art thou young tho' number'd with the dead;
How many mortal generations view'd;
How many more—if time could blanch thy head:
To thine man's life is snow upon the breeze,
More frail beyond compare than e'en the flowers and trees;

VII.

For steadfast thou dost through a cycle stand,
And flow'rs perennially renew their sweets;
But against man is every creature's hand,
He dreams 'tis love and friendship that he meets;
He dies (his loves and friends renew their mirth,)
Remembered no more than if he ne'er had birth.

* Oom al hasn, (Arab.)

VIII.

I saw a woodsman strike his steeled axe
Deep in the shrinking bark of this fair tree,
With blow on blow its ringed trunk he racks,
It shivers through its leaves with agony,
Until its heart the cruel edge did reach,
And all its years of life rush'd wailing through the
 breach.

IX.

As the dull sound rings through the woodlands wide
The silenced birds forsake the doomed oak,
Like men who from the falling great do hide,
When their bright fortunes doth dark ruin cloak :
It groans, then falls—the earth rocks with the sound—
Stretching its broken arms to save it from the ground.

X.

Its rent limbs stand up through the sea of leaves,
That drooping pour their foliage on the earth :
I see thy spoiled beauty and it grieves
My heart to know how vain is all thy worth.
All strength whose root is in the earth must fall ;
But beauty from on high survives the wreck of all.

I.

O Earth ! thy flying vanities I've sung
In all their pictured glory as they pass'd,
Each vision'd ruin still my heart has wrung,
Leaving it dark without a rest at last.

II.

O Man ! on thee whence comes this strong control
To long for, love, the beautiful and bright ?
Is it the aspiration of thy soul
To reach thy God, fount of all beauty's light ?

III.

Yes ; torrent, mountain and the living sea,
And every bird and beast, and man their lord,
And cloud and snow and hail, and flower and tree
Are beautiful, created by His word.

IV.

All beautiful the creatures of His hand,
How many cloth'd with regal majesty,
While some enhaloed in a glory stand,
Some loveliness surrounds with mystery.

V.

But all the beauty thou dost now behold,
Though ravishing to thine imperfect sight,
Yet has a little worm within its fold
Cheating thy human heart with brilliant blight.

VI.

But He who made the beautiful and bright
Can fairer make than eyes e'er gazed upon,
Enrobing it with so resplendent light
'Twould kill the mortal sense on which it shone.

VII.

O God! if Thou who mad'st the beautiful
Canst fairer make, more glorious, more sublime,
After Thy perfect pattern wonderful;
How excellent must Thou in glory shine!

VIII.

What eye of man can dare so dazzling sight?
What words of man can fitly frame Thy praise?
Imagination cannot scale the height
Where happy angels joy in its full blaze.

IX.

For Thou, who mad'st the lovely and the true,
Inspiring them with beauty all above;
What tongue with words Thy glory can indue?
For Thou alone—art Beauty, Truth and Love.

VISIONS

VALLEY OF THE SHADOW OF DEATH.

VISION I.

___

CONSTANCE.

Romeo.—Dost thou not laugh ?
Benvolio.—No, coz ; I rather weep.

What sad thoughts throng my brain as lone I stand,
And muse upon the double life of man ;
The inner wrapt in folds of love and joy,
Or stormy with fierce hate and passion wild :
The outer all hypocrisy or calm,
Till scalding tears, blinding mine eyes, yet fail
My sight to blind, while backward looking far
Across the dark abyss of weary years,
Upon whose shore was cast a shipwreck'd life.
And now I strive to force my listless pen
To fabricate dull lines, while yet I lack
Bright inspiration, like a lightning flash
Gleaming in some crystalline cave, to light
Imagination's gems and clothe my thought.

Time was, when Love wav'd o'er me his young wing,
That burning feelings I could mould in verse,
And waft my gentle tale of hopes and fears
In cadenc'd music to the lov'd one's heart;
For I was one whom pleasure had not pall'd,
Nor Mammon marr'd; and ever did I dream
A dream—how many dream,—of making mine,
Not the ideal of a poet's thought
Or artist's fancy, but a woman true
As last in Eden made by God's own hand,
When the first day, He said, "Let there be light,"
And the last day man's light, fair woman shone,
To glorify the whole.

Hast thou not seen on some dark, stormy night,
When o'er the dreary heath thy steps have pac'd,
And massive clouds in black confusion pil'd
Have chas'd each other 'thwart the troubled sky—
Hast thou not seen some guiding star on high
Shine fitfully; now by dense vapour hid,
Then beaming mildly on thy desert path,
Emerging bright from some chaotic pile,
Till thick'ning vapours one vast curtain form'd
And cloth'd the earth with darkness to be felt?
Thus 'tis in life; Hope's bright but fitful ray
Still glimmering shines, although obscur'd how **aft**

By grief, regret or disappointment's clouds,
Or blighted feelings withering the heart
With misery untold ; yet still we trust
Its pale, deceitful beam, which brighter shines
Contrasted with the darkness spread around,
Luring us onward till despair arise
Casting its mantle dark wide o'er the scene,
And leaving all the soul in rayless gloom.

'Twas before Love wav'd o'er me his bright wing
That on my virgin heart a vision shone,
A vision of exceeding loveliness :——
What 'vails it to recall the Hebe form,
Or splendour of her eyes of halcyon blue,
Hair dark as gilded sunset wave ?   All this,
And more to tell,—oft told,—were to portray
A form ; the deathless spirit to describe
Were to deface :——an all lovely vision,
From whose beauteous presence flow'd a pow'r
My inmost soul compelling to its thrall.
Then first was broken up within my heart
The fountain deep of love : a lambent haze
Of all surpassing light, with diamond sheen
Bathing all earth and bright'ning even heav'n,
Envelop'd my whole being, her enshrin'd
In its pure blaze and rob'd her in its glory :

N

And I worshipp'd her ; such adoration
It surely is no sin ; and she lov'd me !
O ecstasy ! then flew my new-born life
To nestle in her pure and loving heart,
And found a living home of sweetest rest ;
And yet I loved her with a holy love,
Self-sacrificing ; and she loved me
With trust so innocent, that when as oft
Embrac'd we sat, and the deep wordless speech
Well'd from our love-lit eyes and meeting lips,
We fear'd no wrong, for an unearthly charm
Haloed her angel head : within mine arms
She lay, in faith, as in a sanctuary.

But I was poor and she of lowly birth,
Yet surely never was such love as ours ;
Yea truly such love is too pure for earth
And the world's sordid use.   And thus it falls
That no man ever weds his own true wife ;
For since the first transgression ruin'd man
And fall'n woman run a course—not parallel,
Like to unequal wheels whose cogs ne'er meet
But check and jar the whole machinery.
But for this Paradise would be restor'd,
And happy man would seek no other heav'n.

In such a heav'n we liv'd, and still we dream'd
This bliss would last for aye, when suddenly
Came an ill-omen'd summons by a ship
To take her to her home across the sea ;
And thus this great calamity unseen,
And unforeseen, fell with a stunning force
On all our joy : as when a falcon swoops
Plumb down from the cloud's height, the noble bird
Upon the quarry like an arrow falls ;
And with the blow outflash her silver wings
Checking her mad career ; then silent bears
To the crag's point her stunn'd and wounded prey.

But she would not believe that we could part,
It could not be,—so sudden was the blow,
Too deadly to be felt ; but all too soon
The heart's blood follow'd on the steel withdrawn,
And with sensation came the suffering ;
She did not faint, but very pale she look'd,
And clung to me while I to soothe her tried.
O double grief ! to strive a grief to soothe
· From a sad mind fill'd with a greater grief,
When every glozing word the false tongue speaks
The heart abjures.

        " Constance," at length I said.

"Constance, my darling, would you were my wife
But I am poor and so it cannot be.
Would that we two adown the tide of time
Could float together loving and beloved ;
But thus it cannot be ; and we must part."
O ne'er can I erase from memory
The face she rais'd to mine, all marble pale,
With a beseeching agony,

                "O why?

Why say you, love, that we must part ?
' Would that I were ? '   I am your own true wife !
Say not—I cannot speak the killing word."
But in my face she read a mute despair,
And laid her head upon my panting breast,
Murmuring, " Your wife—if not—O your slave—
Still to be with you—live and die for you."

Her bosom heav'd, and 'gainst my side her heart
With passion beat in sorrow uncontroll'd,
And all her hair in rich magnificence
Over her perfect shoulders fell ; curling
Around my hands in mute appeal, to aid
Her deep, deep eyes that turned still to mine
With deepest love, in hope to find some hope !
O beautiful, most beautiful she was

In all her disarray, in all her grief !
O trial for man to bear almost too hard !
While anguish blanch'd my cheek my soul was firm,
Though my lips trembled to destroy her hope,
The last—the last frail plank to which she clung,
" For me to suffer for you were a joy,
To see you suffer more than I could dare :
Alas, my own sweet love, it must not be."
She sunk down fainting, circled in mine arms,
Grief-struck ;—and lay as in a sanctuary.

And the dark time crept on that we must part,
We counted every day, and every hour
As hoarded treasure, and every minute ;
And spent them miserly,—and still they flew,
And made each day a year,—and yet they flew :
At last the dark day came that we must part :
And then we tore each from the other's breast
The fibres that had rooted in our hearts,
And let them bleed ; and kiss'd and parted.

Long, long I watched the bark that bore my life
Away o'er the waving waste, until it sunk
Below the broad ridge of the silent sea ;
Long, long I stood upon the rocks, and felt

The bond that bound me to her tighter drawn,
As waned the ship—tighter and tighter drawn
Till sank the ship ; and then it broke—and parted ;
And with a bitter cry I fell, and there
Drain'd to the utmost dregs the first full cup
Of manhood's anguish ; the chalic'd fire
Scorch'd my young heart ; the bloom of life was gone !
They found me there,—they bore me to my home ;
She was not there !—I never saw her more !

Yet even now my memory looks back
Through the lone vista of my loveless years,
And sees the sunlight gilding all the hills
With purest light : and still my youth's first love
Oft cheers with a sad cheer my lonely heart ;
But the sorrow—the sorrow has been borne !

VISION II.

IÖLÉ.

Lear. Why should a dog—a horse—a rat, have life,
  And thou no breath at all ? O thou wilt come no more.
  Never, never, never, never, never !

O for the Muse of Shakspeare to portray
The course of true love, and the pangs that warp
The surface smooth, and the great joys and woes
That move the glassy essence of man's soul,
His life a plaything on its fickle waves :
As a gay bark, bright sail and banner spread,
Joyous careering through the billowy deep,
Heaves gently to each wave on summer sea,
In beauty and in strength all confident :
Soon on the waters sinks a sullen calm,
Intensely black the dumb sea darkling lies,
Save when illumin'd by the levin's gleam
The steely waste reflects the ship's still form :

Heard distant rolling through the cloudy vault
The volum'd thunder undulating booms ;
And sultry drops fall hissing in the wave,
Shook by the fierce concussion in the skies
From off the coming storm-god's jetty wing :
First sighs the low wind whisperingly, and then
White seething up from the horizon's verge,
Bursts on the fragile bark the unchain'd storm ;
And raging wildly o'er the troubled main
It tears the crest of each opposing wave
Into phosphoric foam to light its track.
Cut into torture by the straining cords,
Roars through the shrouds the lacerated wind,
With deafening scream and scattering aloft
The fragment sails as snow-flakes on the gale :
Unconquer'd on her side she struggling lies,
Her bare arms plunging in the foaming spray
Beneath ; recoiling from th' abyss where sleep
The waters dark, unutterably deep ;
Bravely she rises to the warring shock
Of waters pouring over and around ;
Hope once more gleams, as bounding to the helm
She leaps from wave to wave triumphant.
Vivid ! the lightning strikes her noble hull,
And over all outbursts a thunder peal
Of such magnificence—the howling storm

Seems silence.—No more she strives, but heart-struck
And shuddering through all her frame—slowly
She sinks, while o'er her grave the rampant waves
Ride glorying on, whit'ning the waste with foam.
So love on beauty's bosom softly pillow'd,
Fann'd by the zephyrs with the breath of flowers,
Joys smiling on unweening of the storms
That threat'ning lour to blast his happiness.

O Iölé! all beauteous Iölé!
O that I could enshrine thee in my verse
As thou art shrined in my heart of hearts.
O that I could arrest thy glorious form
In statuary stone; it would be thought
Some goddess by a Grecian chisel wrought,
Dian, or Pallas azure eyed; a form
Canova dreamed yet fail'd to realise.
What were the visions of all poets' souls—
Laura,—sweet Juliet,—queenly Beatrice,—
Spenser's or Tasso's beautiful bright dreams,—
But prophecies—O Iölé—of thee?
'Twas not the dark abundance of her hair,
But all the loves that floated on its waves;
Not the deep purple of her radiant eyes,
But all the loves that sported in their depths;
She was not sweet as rose, or hyacinth,

No, nor as lily fair : they only fair
And sweet in robbing her : surpassing grace
With undulating light cloth'd all her form,
While from her perfect lips with brook-like tone
Sweet music flow'd,—and every breath was hush'd !
But O the charm of her entrancing smile ;
Upon the eye it broke like light restor'd
The blind : such smile illumes an angel's face
Meeting a sorrowing sinner at the gates
Of Paradise.   Love, ere I was aware,
Rush'd like a torrent to my vacant heart ;
I felt the power, yet struggled to be free ;
And then I fled—fled through the world's wide sea :
But the sure net was round me, and ere long
Narrowing its circle broad it brought me back
To where the laughing waves fell happy at her feet :
Within the dark lone mansion of my breast
Long desolate, the lamp of life re-lit
Too grateful burn'd ; and all resistance ceas'd.

And I was silent : yet she could not help
But read the adoration of my soul,
Though rev'rence temper'd love.   And oft my heart
Fill'd up with all I had to tell, and long'd
To give to words the love that master'd me ;
Yet when upon the terrac'd walk we met

In dark seclusion of the chequer'd shade,
And walk'd there side by side, I could not speak :
Deep love is dumb.   And yet she knew it all ;
Heard without words my heart's low murmurings,
And I heard hers ; and to and fro we walk'd
As in a dream : and when she left me there,
My eyes I shut and still I walkèd on,
As she were by my side, and still with her
Held silent converse communing of love :
Though absent yet I felt that she was there,
And heard the rustle of her robes,—and when
Again my eyes I opened, I was sad.
And oft a feeling strange came over me
We two were one, and I felt cloth'd upon
With all her radiant beauty,—her dear eyes
And all her features mine,—till e'en her hair
Fell waving from my brow, and curl'd around
My neck in soft warm folds—all self—all lost !

Long time I lov'd her silently, the hours
How long pass'd near her ; and the days how long ;
For each within its little round contain'd
An age of happiness : yet O how swift,
Swifter than childhood's griefs they pass'd away.
Long time I lov'd her, till it chanc'd one day,
A balmy spring-tide day, from garden toil

Upon a moss'd bank she asleep had fall'n,
O'ershadow'd by an oak tree's wave-green leaves ;
And all around her gather'd flow'rs were strown
Except a few escaping from her hand
Reluctant, weeping pearly tears of dew.
In placid beauty eloquent she lay ;
Her happy life ran through so fair a frame
Rejoicing ; from her parted lips her breath
Fragrance diffused around, and sham'd the flow'rs.

I knelt me down and watch'd her as she slept,
Yet held my breath ; like to a stooping fawn
That in a clear pool sees its own lithe form,
And timid stands at gaze, infascinate
I knelt and watch'd her breathing heave and fall,
And every breath floated its wave of life
Into my inmost soul : and then she woke
And open'd her deep eyes, and did not stir ;
But her eyes dwelt on mine and saw my heart
Unveil'd.   Then slowly rose a roseate blush,
Like to the dawn upon a mountain's snow,
Transfusing her fair face : a little while—
She neither spoke nor mov'd—and I was still,
But gaz'd on that dear face expecting thence
My oracle of happiness or doom.
She half arose and leaned on her hand,

While from her eyes upraie'd two diamond tears
Slowly well'd up, and in her bosom fell :
Then murmuring music broke : " Do you love me ? "
She said ; no more she said.   O what a tide
Of ecstasy from those few little words
Rush'd like a living power through my veins,
And drown'd my breath ; for very happiness
I could not speak, but grasped hard my throat,
Lest my full heart should burst with so great joy—
Joy to the verge of pain ; then by degrees,
Half sighs, my words came forth, " Do I love you ?
Love you ? how madly—O how doatingly !
Love you ? O ask me if I live or breathe ;
Ask the lost trav'ller on the Syrian plain,
Writhing in all the agonising pain
Of parching thirst ; have water would he fain
To cool his blacken'd lips ; ask the cag'd lark
Perch'd on a dead sod in some alley dark,
That sits with quiv'ring wing and upturn'd eye,
And sweetly warbles forth its misery ;
If it would love to soar into the sky,
And bathe its breast in sunbeams ; ask again
Th' imprison'd slave in some dark dungeon pent,
Who daily watches o'er his iron chain,
His nightly dreams on home and freedom bent,
Still waking torture ; whether he would like

From his gall'd limbs to see the links struck off;
And on his darken'd soul hope once more strike
Through his cell's gates unbarr'd—it were to scoff
The miserable with a sight of bliss !—
Love you? too well you know, from the first day
You rose a star upon my night of life,
How I have lov'd you—only liv'd in you."
On her fair hand, so beautiful and soft
That lay in mine, I bath'd my trembling lips :
But then she laugh'd—a little laugh, and said,
" O perjury ! do I not know full well
You've lov'd before ? can any heart love twice ?
Or is it but the pastime of an hour?
I hope 'tis not : I fear 'twould be my death ! "
Her voice sunk low, fearing she'd said too much,
And o'er her glorious eyes the darkling lashes fell,
Veiling their radiance as a cloud the sun.
In holy innocence and truth she spoke,
And nothing false could in her presence live.
" Beloved Iölé, I'll tell you all,
Yea, though I lose your love, I'll tell you all :
O could I with a heart so finely tun'd
To vibrate to the beautiful and high,
Joy in all bright things from the hand of God,
And the most excellent of all His works,
The first link of the chain 'tween earth and heav'n,

Without whom Eden was no paradise,—
Pass unmov'd by ? That I did love, 'tis true,
In the first dawn of life—'twas very brief,
And cross'd :—yet as a gleam of glory
It flashed upon my youth, a foredawn of
The love that thralls me now ; long time I mourn'd,
Mourn'd with the sharp grief of a boyish heart,
For we were parted to meet never more.
But O the difference of love in youth,
And now : then 'twas an all-pervading joy ;
Now, a full, perfect, glorious happiness,
Enduring as my being, one with it,
As I am one with you, my only life :
Tell me, O Iölé—you love me still !"

Upon the grass I lay and kissed her feet,
Her little feet that peepèd from her robe,
And looked up imploringly.   Her eyes
Were fix'd on mine, and drew me with a force
Loving, resistless. .   .   .
Here must I pause and draw a sacred veil
Over that wondrous bliss on earth so rare,
When in the crowd meet two congenial souls
And know their perfect unity fulfill'd.
Love ! holy love ! soul of true poesy !
Ennobling power of weak humanity !

The love of God, of mother, sister, wife,
The love of man and woman, man and man ;
Still must the strain ascend to this clear height,
Or find in human hearts no answering chord.
All other passions that debase the soul
Are only the negations of this love ;
Envy and pride and hate and jealousy,
Revenge and avarice, the absence are
Of the great love inspir'd of God and man,
As darkness is the absence of the sun.
Yet on the earth its pearls I may not pour
Because the trampling herd their beauty strives
To desecrate, and tear with slanderous fang
The hands that loose them from their golden string :
For men there are whom virtue cannot win,
Who scoff at the deep feelings of the soul ;
Who cannot deem of love apart from sin,
Of love divine that through all worlds doth roll :
Like unto wasps that from sweet floral bells
(Where only honey find the balmy bees ;)
Fell poison suck to feed their vengeful stings.

And thus we walk'd together through this vale
Without a grief, our life one gladness all :
Twas in the warm south, where the trellis'd vines
Their festoon'd garlands hang and purple grapes ;

And all the life of nature in the sun
Lies languishing, in a luxurious calm.
One eve, upon a woodland bank reclin'd,
With wild flow'rs all o'ergrown and scented grass :
Th' acacia spread its thick shade overhead,
O'ergemm'd with chains of tassell'd blossoms white,
Like shining lamps : still humm'd the dusty bees
Enflower'd, while flitted the moths around,
Unweening either if 't were day or night,
A twilight shade ; from the far waterfall
Swell'd fitfully the modulated tones.
I heard not the sweet sounds of earth and air,
I saw not if its scenes were dark or fair ;
In Iölé's dear voice all music dwelt,
And all of beautiful the world could give
I saw reflected in her angel eyes.

Reclining by her side, " Dearest," I said,
" In our own land I have a fair abode,
Nestled in woods, from which the grassy slopes
Fall to a river, that through margent meads
Flows winding on, just near enough to waft
To the indweller's ear its varied song.
Here oft in youth I wandered objectless
Along the life-like stream and drank its tones ;
Sometimes it rippled merry roundelays,

Or curling round the pebble stones gave forth
Its bell-like notes, then passed with long low wail
Over subjacent sands.   I wander'd on
Under the bowering trees ; the cushat's voice
Its love moans mingling with the south wind's sob,
And every bird exhal'd its little loves
In melody.   Then dreams came over me
Vague, undefin'd, of joys unrealiz'd :
O how prophetic of my present bliss !
And this sweet home your paradise shall be,
And all that art can do, and nature has,
To make it worthy of thee, shall be thine ;
Music, and pictur'd halls and flowers fair :
And there we'll pass glad weeks of happy days,
And sabbaths happy in the spirèd fane
That points us heavenward.
And at your feet I'll sit and read to you
Poems, and all the riches of men's minds
Treasur'd in books.   Then to sweet toil we'll go,
And watch the rip'ning fruit and plant new flowers.

And at eventide, when the dewdrops glisten
From the trembling boughs, we will sit and listen
To night's lone bird from his leafy dwelling ;
His cadenc'd notes from love's soul upwelling ;
And the sweet brook's rush in music flowing ;

And mark the sky in the far west glowing,
And the ruddy light on the wavelets gleam,
That ring the trout's leap on the glassy stream ;
'Till soars night's queen in her diamond car,
Paling with envy each less'ning star.

O then away to some ruin grey,
Where the gothic arch and column tall
Solemnly rear'd against her pallid ray,
Black in the moonlight loom,
Mingling their shades with the ivied wall ;
And th' owlet's wing round turret and hall
Flits in the darkling gloom.
How sweet to roam the greenwood shade,
And watch the full fair moon :
No sound from out the forest glade
Ruffling the night's dark plume ;
While the distant swell of waters fell
Like the sound —
            Iölé, you weep ! "
" Oh yes : I cannot help but weep, to think
This scenic vision beautiful as frail,
With skyward pointing towers may all dissolve
Before the poison blasts of daily use,
Or sudden fall and whelm us in its fall."

Like a storm cloud across a spotless sky
Her words swept over me : but then she laugh'd ;
And all her tears like drops of dew at morn
Were drièd in the sunshine of her smile.
" Beloved, am I not all thine ? " she said,
" With you I'll go to your fair paradise,
And strive to realize your fancy's dreams ! "

O morn of joy ! with Iölé my bride :
All glorious in her beauty as she shone ;
O day of rapture ! when I call'd her mine ;
Mine—mine all : embraced we stood ; our two hearts
Tun'd to one music beat in unison ;
Like twin stars in the galaxy we stood,
In mystery of all effulgent light ;
[Rather like glory trailing meteors
That light their own track through the midnight sky,
Then die, and all is dark.]
                              Then playfully,
" Go now," she said, " for we must quick prepare
To take our journey to our distant home."
Recall'd to earth—I look'd around, and there—
Boxes half pack'd, papers and books and arms :
I kiss'd her and unwillingly went forth ;
Like a young girl who bears a precious vase
I trembled at imaginary ills,
While rapt in joy too deep for utterance ;

How little could I know that lingering kiss
Was the last seal of so much happiness!

I heard a dull sound as of something fallen—
My heart stood still,—a sudden shot,—and then
Came mingled with my name a sharp quick cry,
Back to the room I flew.   Horror! O horror!
The stand whereon a case of arms had stood
Was on the floor; a white cloud stole aloft:
Merciful Heav'n! did ever man endure
Horror so dread, and live?   There—there she lay—
My Iölé—my bride—bleeding she lay—
And in her beautiful white throat a wound,
A little wound weeping her precious blood,
Her life,—her very life!   The maniac shriek
Rose to my throat and strove for utterance;
'Twas strangled there!   Madness must have follow'd
Upon speech: Yet it strove to master me,—
My heart was rending with the agony;
My brain with anguish unfathomable
Totter'd and reel'd: ages of bitterness
Were in the cup I drain'd.
                              I knelt by her,
She breath'd,—and once she open'd her dear eyes,
And smil'd on me: O smile seraphic!
I see it still!—I took her in my arms

And press'd her lips to mine,—until they grew
Cold,—O so cold,—so cold,—and she was dead !—
Gently I laid her down,—her bridal veil
All dyèd with her blood : and still I gaz'd,
For I could not believe that she was dead :—
So glorious a life,—it was impossible,—
So sudden,—to cease to be.   Her cagèd bird
Pour'd forth a strain that madded me, and liv'd !
And I arose ; and there were faces round,—
Faces of men, with life !—of common men—
And women,—and they lived, for some wept !
But she—O Iölé—wife—angel—Oh !
Not dead—not dead—not dead !

                               I could no more :—

The blood was freezing in my veins ; the crash
Of worlds was in my brain ; the ocean's roar
Was pouring through mine ears ; and on my sight
Darkness !—then silence all !

                               Like unto one
That wakes upon the resurrection morn,
And hears the bursting of the sepulchre,
The rending earth, all mingled with the shout
Of the Archangel, and the mighty rush
Of myriads, each rising with his spoil ;
So by degrees,—with jarring sound confus'd,

And flashing light—'woke my bewilder'd sense ;
And consciousness brought back a dull dead pain ;
My hand knew not my face ; 'twas chang'd as if
Old age o'erleaping intervening time
Had cast its snows upon me.   Then memory
Restor'd the awful vision of that day
Brought back : but I was calm, the storm had pass'd.
So when the proud oak's crest the levin bolt
Strikes,—its strong heart piercing with liquid fire,
Its giant limbs splinter and crash and rend,—
While still the solid trunk unscathèd seems :
Yet year by year, the blow hollows unseen,
Until a barkèd shell is all that stands
To fall to the woodman's axe.   Thus this shock,
Shattering both head and limb, had left a grief, —
A life-long grief to eat into the heart,
And leave to death a barren victory.

I.

Why art thou gone? my beautiful, my life!
Was there no meaner life for death to slay?
Why art thou gone? my beautiful, my wife!
Had loveliness no power his hand to stay?

II.

It makes me mad to think that thou art gone,
And all the earth to me is dark and frore:
Yet in the darkest watch of night all lone,
I see thy radiant form mine eyes before.

III.

When my brain aches to burst its burning zone,
And reason hovers o'er the dread abyss;
I sometimes think my heart will turn to stone,
Far better so,—than suffering like this.

IV.

And dost thou think of me and love me still
In that pure heav'n more meet for thine abode?
To know thou dost would shield my soul from ill,
And from my bosom ease this heavy load.

V.

Oh, if I thought I should not see thee more,
I could not bear this weary life to keep :
O no, to angels thou art gone before
To glad their hearts, lest they for me should weep.

VI.

Yes, I shall see and love thee evermore,
Without love heav'n is robb'd of its pure light :
For heav'n itself is love ;—the living air
That angels breathe among their bowers bright.

VII.

Again I turn to earth,—I see thee not!
Why art thou gone? my beautiful, my life!
Gone is my life! then heart why break'st thou not?
Why art thou gone? my beautiful, my wife!

VISION III.

MOTHER'S LOVE.

A mother's love !   O 'tis a heavenly light,
'Twas never kindled at an earthly shrine ;
The child's ingratitude, neglect and slight
Oft brighter make th' immortal flame to shine.

A mother's love !   O 'tis a guardian spirit,
With waiting wings watching o'er youth's career,
The lov'd ones shielding from the ills they merit,
While weeping o'er their sins with many a tear.

And when the man she is no longer nigh,
Her presence still dwells with him like a charm ;
He hears the dear name with a deep-drawn sigh,
A mother's love still saves his soul from harm.

Onward it goes with him toward the tomb;
When other ties forsake, or break, or sleep,
It thrills his heart with thoughts of childhood's home,
And at his mother's name the aged man will weep.

I see a vision sad before me rise,
A fair child dying on a bed of sorrow;
Slumber has closèd up his pale fring'd eyes,
Fell pain his frail form has forgot to harrow.

And by her darling, lo! his mother dear;
The breaking dawn upon her sweet face smil'd
As to her God she mov'd her lips in prayer,
Deep, fervent, loving, for her dying child.

" O Thou most High who seest my utter grief,
Father of mercies, grant my child relief;
O hear my cry; Thou only hast the power
To succour when the clouds of peril lour.
Thou at the foot of the accursed tree,
Where Mary knelt in speechless agony,
Beheld'st a mother's heart by anguish riven,
O hear a mother's prayer; Hear me God in Heaven.
Over my head let all Thy billows pour;
But spare, O spare my child in this dread hour;

Save his lov'd form from racking torments fierce,
And through my heart let all Thine arrows pierce.
Ah me, what words are these?—O God, forgive,
Nor in Thy memory let my rash words live,
Forgive a mother's prayer—that prays for one
Dearer to her than life,—Father, Thy will be done!"

She rose from off her knees, gaz'd on her child,
And stooping listened to his gentle breath,
And felt a timid hope he might be spared;
Weary with watching him at length she slept.

A strain sweet, exquisite, as 'twere the soul
Of music freed from earthly instruments,
Bath'd all her being in its melody;
Then a bright spirit pass'd before her face
The shape whereof she then could not discern,
Arrayed all in white, resplendent wings
Diaphonous above its shoulders shone,
And lambent light play'd all around its form;
Then it stood still; then passèd onward forth.
As motion'd by its will she seemed to 'rise
And follow silently; they passed through
A crowd of children busy with their games,
Happy as on some joyous holiday;
Until she came to a lone prison room,

And there she saw a fair-hair'd boy who sat
Sobbing convulsively; within his arms
Buried his face; while on his back was seen
A label written thus, " Liar and thief."
Long, long he sobb'd as though his heart would break,
For while he heard the joyful throng below,
For him there was no hope of liberty.
And then his mood was chang'd, he clench'd his hands,
And lifting up a wrath-distorted face,
The mother saw the likeness of her son !
She turn'd away; that bright one onward mov'd;
And weeping sad, sad tears, she follow'd on:
They passed through a lighted gorgeous room
Where men and women sat, drank and blasphem'd
And sang their ribald songs, and play'd for gold.
All this in shielded innocence she saw
As through a veil; until she stood within
A room, where on a couch a fair-hair'd youth
Pillow'd his head upon a harlot's lap,
Inebriate, his arm across his face
He slumber'd restlessly.   O piteous sight
To see so noble creature so defac'd :
The woman spoke, and when from off his face
He toss'd his arms, still beautiful though fall'n,
The mother saw the likeness of her son !
She turn'd away; onward that bright one mov'd :

Weeping most bitter tears she follow'd on.

They passed through a crowd that choked up

The folding portals of a judgment hall;

The husht throng parting as she enter'd in.

A little while she stood; then heard a voice

In solemn tones above the silent crowd

Pronouncing on a blood-bespotted man

The awful sentence of his earthly doom;

And in the midst a man of noble form

Stood in a void spot, horror on his brow,

Alone, environ'd by a great despair!

The mother turn'd and look'd upon his face,

And saw once more the likeness of her son!

She saw no more! deep grief had dried her tears.

Then softly stole upon her spirit's sense

The same pure melody, sweet, heavenly,

Her wounded spirit healing with a balm,

Her sad face smoothing with celestial calm,

Within whose effluence no grief could live.

That bright one stood before her; from his form

Beam'd light seraphic, and she veil'd her eyes;

Then there was silence, and she heard a voice,

" More just shall mortal man be than his God?

Lo! in His Seraphim He put no trust,

Then how much less in those that dwell in dust:

They perish, none regardeth, and they die

E'en without wisdom." " But none considereth
That the righteous from the evil days to come
Are ta'en away." Behold!

                She rais'd her eyes
Unto that bright one's face all glorified,
Until its beams had ceas'd to dazzle her;
In his blue eyes the light of heav'n shone,
And waves of heaven's light upon his hair,
In very truth the mother knew her child;
And then he parted from her with a smile,
An angel smile, murmuring " Mother dear!"
Again the strain, celestial music breathing,
Caught the gentle words, and interwove them
With its harmony; and then it faded
In cadenc'd echoes from eternal space,
Still whispering fainter, lower, " Mother dear!"
Until it died away. Her loving heart
Was full fill'd with an ecstasy of joy;
She started from her sleep; her child was dead!
I saw her weep—O yes—she needs must weep;
And then with streaming eyes she murmured,
" O joy in woe—Father, Thy will be done!"

              The Sun had risen

VISION IV.

THE OLD MAN'S PLAINT.

I.

Lost ! lost ! life lost ! I look'd back on the past,
And all that I had borne of grief and pain ;
And while I thought how hard my lot was cast,
No discontent within my heart did reign ;
I bore the burden of the heavy day,
Not stooping to complain nor ask Time's hand to stay.

II.

My youth's first love pass'd as a flash away,
Leaving a glory where its light had been ;
My manhood's trust prov'd but a form of clay,
Whelm'd in life's turbid flood—a loveless dream.
I steel'd my breast against the shafts of life,
Not caring for its barbs nor shrinking from its knife.

III.

'Tis true that griefs had lured me to sin,
And on the brink of ruin dark Despair
Had strongly urged me to plunge within,
And end my sufferings in her sullen lair ;
On floating wrecks of faith I scap'd the snare,
Or by God's grace was sav'd in answer to my prayer.

IV.

I thought 'twas peace until I saw thee come,
A bright soul gemm'd with jewels not of earth ;
A vision beautiful, whose glory shone
With darkening radiance on all lower worth ;
Then came the fiery trial hard to bear,
Heating the iron bonds I'm doom'd for life to wear.

V.

For thou art not a creature of the brain,
Though come too late my wearied heart to mock ;
Fair flow'r of earth, nurtur'd with heavenly rain,
Tho' storm bow'd as the hare-bell on the rock ;
Yet if that rock is Christ, cast off thy fears,
For God's most blessed fruit is watered by tears.

VI.

'Tis not the thought of troubles past and gone,

Unkindnesses that sear the heart and life;

'Tis not the thought of suffering I have borne,

The inner hopelessness, the outward strife;

But now that thou my evening path hast cross'd,

It is the thought—the thought of all that I have lost.

VII.

Yet all is peace; though sever'd here below,

Where man's ordeal is to be heart-lone,

There is a painless life where love shall flow

In measureless effulgence from God's throne.

There shall all meet, no longer trial-toss'd;

The lost ones they have lov'd, the lov'd ones they have

    lost!

The Visions fade behind us as we pass
Onward to where the light breaks through the gloom,
Where ends the Valley of the Shade of Doom,
Through which Thy staff the Pilgrim guided has.
Now on his sight the glorious light doth gain,
Brighter than that which shone at broad mid-day
Round holy Paul, when journeying on the way ;
Its splendour waxing as the world doth wane ;
Pouring its radiance on the mossy grave,
Where angels wait, depute by love most blest
To waft the spirit to its happy rest,
Where Jesus dwells Omnipotent to save.
Now can he smile unmov'd on sorrows past,
And realise the bliss that shall for ever last.

MISCELLANEOUS.

CHARITY.

An incident in the Life of Lord Herbert of Cherbury.

———

All joy had fled the village; silence reign'd;
For locust-like the host at early morn
Had passed o'er the land, and the bright spot
Nestling so lovely in its fields of corn,
And garlanded about with trees that watch'd
Their chequer'd shadows in the brook below,
Was scath'd by murd'rous rapine's searing brand,
And all its glory marr'd. A space apart
Upon the mountain's side a mansion rose,
Whose portals open lay to all the winds;
And desolate within a woman sat
Beside her desecrated hearth. Her eye
Was fix'd on vacancy, and dry with grief;
Tearless and beautiful as Niobe,
She knew not if her husband were in bonds,

Or slain; and still the infant on her lap
In her sad face laugh'd joyously.   In vain
She sat and listen'd to each sound—attent
For helping voice of neighbour, friend,—in vain;
For all had suffer'd equally with her,
And could no comfort to another bring.

Lord Herbert rode across the weary land,
He and his squire on service of his King;
And faint he was with hunger as he rode,
For they had two days travell'd without food.
And when the house upon the mountain slope
He came before, he rode up to the gate
Where desolate within the woman sat.
Thus had she sat till eventide; when lo,
The sound of arms and horses; and she said,
" Behold the spoilers are return'd."   Howbeit
Unto the door she mov'd, and then she saw
Without, a mounted knight of noble mien.
Saluting her right courteously, he said,
" Fair dame, I've travell'd fasting since the eve:
If you have bread or food within the house,
For God's sake, or for money, succour us."
Lifting her eyes unto the speaker's face
As one that dream'd, " This morn, my lord," she said,
" The ruthless soldiery pass'd through the land

And left—hunger and woe, but neither bread nor food:
And ye that are their lords are much to blame,
That curb them not from rapine and from crime:
You come in evil hour." She turn'd away,
And passed in; and on a broken bench
Sat with her babe beside her ruin'd hearth.
Lord Herbert mused a little, and then said,
" Princes in sooth should care for this, who raise
This beast of prey to prowl at large the earth,
And keep him not enchain'd; a bitter scourge
Alike to friend and foe: meanwhile the pangs
Of hunger rend me, fasting since so long."
To whom his squire, " I marvel you believe
This woman; I will search in byre and barn
For hidden stores, and doubt not soon to find
Wherewith to remedy our hunger pains."
And so he went. And the Lord Herbert pass'd
Into the house and sadly sat him down,
For he was faint to death; and looking round
He saw the bare walls, and the sanded floor
With rough feet rippled, as by a cross tide;
A wreck of broken vessels; arras torn;
Panel with dint of axe; fire-blacken'd log,
And household stuff in vex'd confusion thrown;
And 'mid the ruin, nursing her sweet babe,
The woman by her desolated hearth.

A lovely sight,—a mother with her child,

Feeding her lov'd one with her own dear life.

A lovely and a holy sight it is,

And strongly binds our human sympathies;

So strongly binds,—that the old heathen world

And the one half of modern Christendom

Have shrined her in idolatry.   Pondering

She sat, and in his face look'd wistfully,

And saw a noble nature in sore strait;

For he had sunk in faintness to the earth.

And she arose, and said, "As God is judge

My lord I told you truth; I have no food."

And then she paus'd, while pity's angel tears

Rose to her eyes, and a celestial blush

Rob'd her in modesty.   "Methinks," she said,

" I cannot bear to see so noble knight

Fainting for want; I with like suffering

Can feel for you; but I can still await

Until aid from some neighbour household come;

Or if not, I can lay me down and die.

But God has bless'd me with this infant's food

Abundantly, and I will press my bosom's milk

Into this cup to allay your present pain."

And then she waiting stood with downcast eyes,

Rob'd all in modesty, while the sweet babe

Its dimpled arms stretch'd out and crow'd consent.

Lord Herbert gazed upon her blushing face
With reverence and wonder; and the pangs
Of suffering were in his vitals still'd,
And in his strong man's breast deep thoughts rose up,
Thoughts that had almost melted him to tears.
He leapt upon his feet, though weak, and said,   .
" O noble woman, this your gracious offer
Has sham'd the pain from out my coward frame,
And given me strength to brave the onward way.
If he, who for Christ's sake cold water gives,
Fail not of his reward, what shall be thine?
This charity of thine outblazons far
The loftiest stories of antiquity.
The Roman fed her father from her breast,
And sav'd his life to whom she owed her own:
But thou wouldst save a stranger; and he too
One that thou think'st has wrong'd thee.   If for her
A temple rose to filial piety;
How much more worthy were it to build up
A temple here to Christian charity.
God bless thee, and thy child; and God forefend
That I should rob it of its sustenance.
But let me kneel and kiss your bounteous hand,
In homage to your great and generous heart:
And evermore as I pass on my way,
Among all knights and princes I'll proclaim

That, in my wanderings throughout the world,
The most heroic charity I've found
Was this of thine." He kiss'd the babe; and knelt,
And kiss'd her hand: and then rode fasting forth
Through the dark hours; and from the nearest place
Where help was found, he sent help for her need;
Where still the noble woman, with her child,
Sat mourning 'mid the ruins of her home.

EGERIA.

A solemn shade ! The forest trees rear up
Their columns round the marge of the dark pool
In which they fall revers'd; the boughs above
A canopy of densest foliage hang,
Leaf answering to leaf, and flow'r to flow'r,
And every woven branch reflected back
In crystal shrin'd : while downward pour
Willows in weeping masses lanceolate,
And meet their fellows in the polish'd pool.

When at high noon the sun has clear'd the rocks
And trees that bound with deepest shade the space,
Like fragments of a mirror, here and there
The gleams of light sparkle and pass away ;
Or arrowy pillars pierce with falling lines
The waters dark meeting the rays in air.

Silence should be ; but from the basin's edge
A wild young stream leaps down a rocky glen,
Its music echoing through the sombre hall,
Roof'd and festoon'd with curtains ever green ;
The banks around are cloth'd with softest turf,
But the wild flow'rs for want of light look pale,
And on their weak stalks droop : the ousel shy
Upon the stone sits still and dares not dip
Into the solid jet, but cautiously
It casts its bright eye round, and then flies off
To where is heard th' escaping water's voice.

Under the trees, within the farthest gloom
Where in the bottom of a shallow well
A living fountain bubbl'd from the sand,
Embroider'd round with balsams white and fern,
A couch arose, of trefoil soft and moss,
All carpeted about with flowers fair.
Here stood Egeria ! reveal'd by her own light
Which glorious shone athwart the verdant hall,
And like a sunset on th' horizon's verge
Illum'd one half the pool with soften'd glow :
Her tabled brow as marble white was writ
With wisdom heav'nly ; her parted hair
Flow'd down on either side in solid fall,
And at her shoulders stopp'd like water turn'd

By a smooth rock abrupt, nor further roll'd :
Her purple eyes, or cast down deep in thought
Tinging the fring'd transparent lids with blue,
Or cast aloft, and from their star-ray'd light
Around her perfect face a halo shed.
Her arms of roseate alabaster mov'd
With solemn grace, as sway'd her mind her thoughts :
Unzonèd to her feet a spotless robe
Adown her noble stature waving fell,
Save where uplifts its folds the bosom's swell
In purest beauty's undulating lines.
Three times she pac'd with slow and flowing steps
Around the green banks of the darkling lake
With motion musical ; and then she paus'd
And on the couch reclin'd, a being godlike !

And now above the stillness of the woods
A foot approaches, and with prideful tread
The Sabine chief, usher'd by zephyrs wing'd
That rough the surface of the sleeping pool
In manly majesty before her comes :
His bright young brow unhelmeted, his eyes,
Subdued their eagle fire, were fix'd upon
Her face with deepest reverence and love ;
The whispering trees quiver'd with kindred joy.
She rais'd her eyes inspir'd, her beauteous lips,

Arch'd like love's bow, parted; and then a flash
Like the reflection faint from a blown rose
Over her features pass'd: then a clear voice
Which vibrated each tense chord of his soul,
" Stoop down : " he knelt, and leaning from her couch
She kiss'd his lips.   The Earth had pass'd away !
And with his heavenly guide his spirit freed
Was borne to the Elysium of the Gods.

THE NIGHTINGALE.

Hail, fairy bird ! if bird thou art,
And not a spirit sent on earth
From realms of woe, with burning heart,
Or fields of bliss, where joy has birth.
Hail, fairy thing ! wafted on angel wing,
Pouring thy joys and woes in liquid song,
Whether at night, upon the moonlit trees,
Or midday warm, warbling the shades among.
    Hark ! how it rises—up and up—
        Thrilling clear ;
    Then sinks in startling plaintive fall,
        Low and near ·
Now droning dreamily a dulcet symphony ;
Then rolling recklessly in rippling harmony,
Or bubbling o'er in daring melody ;
        As torrent strong
        Rushing along,
An anguish'd scream, telling of fears ;
Then a low wail, melting to tears :

A deep, deep roll,

As though its soul

Went gushing out from its bursting throat

In mellifluous waves of sound :

Then sweeping round

Once more it soars,

Wreathing eddies bright

Of corruscated light ;

Leaping, flashing in a flame of song ;

While joy on joy, and woe on woe,

The glorious tones prolong,

Upwelling from its heart, from off its silver tongue.

Sudden it stops.   With uplifted hand

Under the moon I see Silence stand,

Listening attent in suspensive pain,

Until once more outpours the soul-absorbing strain.

BABYLON.

'Tis midnight : and is heard throughout the camp
Nought but the creaking of the camels' teeth,
As on the sand they ruminating lie,
Waving their phantom necks in the red glow
Of dying watch-fires ; or the dreaming neigh
Of restless weary steeds ; while scatter'd sleep
Dark Arab forms wrapt in their mantles' folds ;
And on the goats' hair tents the flickering ray
Beams ruddy, casting into deeper shade
The gloom beyond, and stamping on the mind
A scene impressive, that in after times
Will rise on harass'd memory's raptur'd eye
Like a faint flash from a forgotten dream.
As over nature hangs a solemn pall,
I wander forth into the silent night,
Whose arched dome with emerald worlds all hung
Awes by its vast immensity ; while o'er

The pathless waste come sighing the soft winds
Complainingly, wafting through solitude
In floating murmurs to the soothed ear
The moaning of the waters, like the wail
Of spirits whispering before a storm.
And as I roaming muse upon the grave
Entombing proud Assyria's city queen,
The jackals' mournful howls come startlingly
From out their ruinous haunts, where demon-like
They crouching lie, and on the crushed heart
Of a once mighty empire seem preying ;
Where erst was heard the roar of myriads
Vibrating on ether ; as pouring burst
Forth from her hundred brazen gates her bands
Of warriors steel'd in gorgeous panoply,
Making the firm earth quiver with the shock
Of fierce horse hoofs and rushing chariot wheels.
As on the height of Baal's scathed fane,
Of God's eternal truth dark monument,
Awe-struck I stand, just as the glowing moon
Scatt'ring the mist in which she pillow'd rose,
Looks down in light upon Euphrates' stream,
Revealing all her might and pride laid low.
Not all thy pillar'd pomp, great Babylon,
Palace and temple proudly pile on pile
Rising in shadowy grandeur to the skies ;

Nor power, when thou rear'dst thy haughty crest,
Enthroning blasphemy upon thy brow,
And marshall'd millions to obey thy will
Rush'd palpitating, could a feeling raise
To equal the sublimity of this
Thine utter desolation.   Or ever
From thy stupendous walls was loos'd a stone,
When nought could check the open scornful smile
Upon the lip of incredulity ;
When in the zenith of thy glory thou
Stood'st confident, the fiat had gone forth
In sounds of woe promulgating thy doom !
And now where are ye, conquerors and kings,
That wav'd your banners o'er the subject earth ?
Where art thou, queen of nations, that didst blast
With dark idolatry the souls of men ?
Where art ?
But on my solitary ear my words
Fall mockingly.   For from the echoless
And undulating waste no voice replies !

A BALLAD.

The boat lay across the ferry,
The lights shone under the trees,
And the lady's laugh was merry,
The bright clouds flew on the breeze.

The knight by the water waited,
His heart leapt glad at the sound ;
And the moon shone on his corslet,
His shadow fell on the ground.

But soon the dark clouds came over,
And the moon it shone no more,
He heard the oars faintly plashing,
The lady had left the shore.

Sharp gusts swept down the ferry,
The skiff it fearfully roll'd,
The lady's train so merry
Was more than it well could hold.

The knight strain'd into the darkness,
And his charger snorted loud ;
A shriek drown'd the oars' faint plashing,
And the moon look'd through a cloud.

The knight and horse the next minute
Were flashing across the stream ;
In vain they swam, both horse and man ;
The moon shone with fainter gleam.

Smoothly flow'd the rushing river
Where the little boat had been ;
A feather lay on the water,
But no living thing was seen.

On the fisher's cot they laid her,
She look'd like a saint at rest ;
One hand lay heavy by her side,
The other lay on her breast.

Her lovely form and sweet pale face,
As mournfully they stand,
Seem'd a white figure on a tomb
Cut by a sculptor's hand.

The torch blaz'd high, the knight stood by,
Deep anguish chok'd his breath ;
He gazed hard upon her face,
As though it were not—death.

And then he took her in his arms ;
Upon his cold mailed breast
Her fair head lay, as a dead child's
Might on its dead mother's rest.

Over the bright steel flow'd her hair,
His brow wore a grief-wrung frown ;
And then he kiss'd her forehead fair,
Then he gently laid her down.

'Twas dark ; he lay upon her grave,
And mus'd on the water deep ;
He thought 'twould quench his burning brain
To die and with her sleep.

His eye was dry, his heart was stone ;
Then he tore the turf and rav'd,
A curse was rising to his tongue
Against God who might have sav'd.

Then came a low voice on his soul
As the voice of the loved dead ;
He heard the words but not the sound,
And most lovingly it said,

" The Lord hath given," thus it said,
" And He may take away :
Weep not for me ; I am with God ;
But turn to Him and pray.

So shall we meet in Heav'n's bliss
Where no grief can abide,
And love through all eternity,
Through Him who for us died."

Then his iron heart was melted,
And bent his iron knees,
The tempter strong within his soul
Still struggled for his fees ;

But the thought of his saint in Heav'n
Over his spirit crept,
He lifted up his face to God,
And pray'd to Him and wept.

With their edges ting'd with glory
The clouds passed one by one;
And looking down from its starry throne
The moon it calmly shone.

THE PLAINT OF THE EXILE.

Sad! sad! sad! on my brain the thoughts ring out
Like the dull tolling of the passing bell;
The while I turn my weary eyes about
In the vain search for those I love so well.

They've pass'd away, and I am left all lone;
They've pass'd away, and my heart weeps for them;
Did I say weep? mine eye is dry as stone;
Such drops the dying plant weeps from its broken stem.

My wife! have I a wife? O dearest why,
Why dost thou rise my sight to curse and bless?
To bless as with a vision from on high,
To curse with thoughts of our lost happiness?

Your dear lov'd face paling with silent grief
I see : I see your loving arms outspread,
While my heart aches to fly there for relief,
Yet still the years ebb on and blanch my head.

Wait, wait, O Time, nor dim her glorious form ;
O Time, touch not her hair, nor thin her cheek ;
Cast down the giant oak that braves the storm,
But gently, gently pass o'er one so fair and meek.

Yet why should Time stand still where hope is none ?
Long years have pass'd, long years will pass again,
And I a broken exile still drag on,
Rusting with tears of blood my iron chain.

And thou my child, my lost my darling child,
I well recall your laughing eyes of blue ;
They tell me now that you are loving, mild,
And fair of feature and of nature true.

Yet not for me to lead your maiden feet,
No, not for me to teach your soul aspire ;
Strangers will reap your smiles, your heart will meet
Strangers with my love, my kiss, your banish'd sire.

And shall I never clasp you to my heart,
Nor lavish on you all a father's love?
No, from mine eye no tear of joy must start;
O grant me strength to bear it, God above.

The grass fades and renews, the trees let fall
Their leaves, and joy returns to them in spring;
Year echoes blank year dead and joyless all;
To me until death come no change they bring.

Sad! sad! sad! on my brain this monotone
Falls like the tolling of the passing bell;
The while my soul sends forth its bitter moan
All desolate for those I love so well.

A SONG OF PRAISE.

The Earth is mine, albeit I know that men
Hold princedoms, realms, and kingdoms on its crust ;
The Earth is mine, with all its gold and gems ;
With all its mountains, rivers, seas, and dust ;
And I will use them to adorn the shrine
Of Him, The Living God, Who made them mine.

The Heavens are mine, with all their stars and suns ;
The Universe is mine, with all its host :
I hear through all a harmony that runs,
Sphere answering to sphere, each striving most
With music sweet to exalt high God's great name,
Making the vast of space melodious with His fame.

In thought I go back to the birth of things,
When light upon the darkness first arose,
And this huge globe, as on majestic wings,
Roll'd through lone space, concentric beds of ooze,
When at the fiat of His sovran will
Upburst the fractured earth in mountain, gulf and
    hill.

Plung'd down the cavern'd deeps the waters pour,
Hurl'd seething back from th' incandescent mine
With 'ruption dire, and volum'd vapours hoar,
Hurtling enormous hail of boulders crystalline,
That shower'd o'er the waste, and cooling in its fall,
Has form'd throughout all time the ocean's rolling
    wall.

Leaping with new-found life from rock to rock,
The sheeted torrents through the valleys fling
Their turbid waves : with earth-appalling shock,
Vast cataracts from off the mountains spring,
" The multitudinous seas " at His command,
Collecting in their place, spread broad from land to
    land.

Embedded in the slime the Saurian old,
Sudden arrested by the mighty drain,
With plunging claws and scaly writhing fold,
Its prey half-swallow'd, strives to 'scape in vain ; *
Fix'd at His word by all petrifick power,
Reptile, fish, and shell, stand perfect to this hour.

The dried-up land is cover'd with a pall
Of green and gold, of leaf, and fruit, and flower ;
And graceful creatures roam the forests tall,
And under brightest bloom the reptiles cower ;
Flash on the virgin air the colour'd birds,
And with melodious notes pour forth their praiseful
          words.

The mountain tops lift up their heads to Thee,
And magnify Thy name with voice of storms;
The clouds hang round in darkling majesty,
And praise Thy name in thunder ; while the forms
Of nimble lightnings, to extol it higher,
Pour through the cloudy vault rivers of furrow'd fire.

------

  * See Collection of Fossil Reptiles, &c. in the Museum at
Bath.   All organic remains prove the suddenness of the change
by which they were preserved.

Through all the woods and forests of this globe,
That clothe it with infinity of leaves :
And plants that gird it with a gorgeous robe ;
'Mid all this sea of leaves that Nature weaves,
No leaf resembles leaf—despite of chance—
For Thou hast made them all Thy glory to enhance.

The myriad creatures of the earth and sands,
And countless thousands on each leaf that dwell,
And in each water drop ; these unseen bands,
With limbs and faculties perfected well ;
These glorify Thy name from hour to hour,
Yet are these but—" the hiding of Thy power."

To Thee who made of worlds th' unnumber'd throng,
And launch'd them forth on their harmonious race,
What is this earth ? a grain the sands among
An atom floating through unbounded space :
Yet hast Thou stooped from Thy throne of light,
To care for this Thy work and glorify Thy might.

R.

Thou art fairer than the silver sheen,
That lights the placid sea beneath the moon ;
And grace, as pearl drops from the deep serene,
Flows from Thy lips : the sun at highest noon
Is not so glorious to my outward sense,
As to my soul Thy love's magnificence.

Gladness before Thee walks with silent spell,
And smiles upon the sorrows of our race ;
With ear attent, as one for music's swell,
Hearing the wondrous triumphs of God's grace ;
And Joy, her twin, with eyes on heav'n that dwell,
Laughing at all terrors born of death and hell.

And Charity, enveiled in snow-white stole,
Kneels at Thy feet and raises loving eyes ;
While down her cheek the priceless tear-drops roll,
Imploring pardon for Thine enemies.
Lo ! at the smile of the Incarnate Word,
Justice unveils,—-and sheathes the unavenging sword.

And shall I form a crown for Thee of Thine ?
Of every jewel treasured in the sand ?
Fair diamonds that with truthful brilliance shine,
Pure amethyst, and royal emerald bland,
Deep hopeful sapphire, ruby's zealous flame,
Wreath'd with finest gold, such as cunning artists
    frame.

Oh, no ! for when a radiant diadem
I've fram'd—to deck the brow of earthly king,
How in Thy splendour jewel, gold, and gem
Fade ; and behold a vain and worthless thing,
That in the shadow of Thy glory faints,
Even unmeet to crown the least of all Thy saints :

For they wear crowns of Thy all perfect light.
How shall unhallow'd lips Thy glory sing ?
How can frail tongue enword such theme aright ?
Imagination droops on airless wing,
All numbers fail to speak the thoughts that spring ;
The hand that strikes the harp rests fix'd upon the
    string.

All glory, majesty, and might are Thine !
No thought can reach a height so high as this ;
No splendour can above Thy splendour shine :
Thou art the Sum of all—the Crown of bliss !
And all their crowns Thy glorious creatures fling
Beneath Thy throned feet, the only crownless King.

GASTON DE FOIX.

THE EARL OF FOIX.

GASTON, *his Son, brought up in the household of the* PRINCE OF WALES.

EVAIN DE FOIX, *Gaston's bastard brother.*

THE BLACK PRINCE.

THE PRINCESS OF WALES.

THE DUKE OF ANJOU.

THE DUKE OF NAVARRE.

COUNTESS OF FOIX.

ISABEL D'ARMAGNAC, *in the household of the Princess.*

SIR JOHN FROISSART.

THE BASTOT DE MAULÉON
SIR AIMERY } *Captains of free lances.*

SIR ERNALTON OF BÉARN.

JOSSELIN
HALBERT } *Falconers.*

RAYMONET DE L'EPÉE, *Retainer of* FOIX.

ARNULPH, BASIL, *Retainers of* D'ARMAGNAC.

PAULINE, *waiting-woman.*

SCENE.—*The South of France, A.D. 1360.*

GASTON DE FOIX.

—o—

ACT I.

SCENE 1.—*Tarbes. The Court of the Castle.*

Enter THE PRINCE, THE PRINCESS OF WALES, THE
EARL OF FOIX, GASTON, ISABEL, *Attendants,
Huntsmen and hounds, Falconers and hawks.*

PRINCE. We are much grac'd, my noble lord of Foix,
By this visit; proving an open faith
And the amity you've ever borne us,
Which from one of so high worth we value.

EARL. My merit being the bright offspring of
Your highness' courtesy, is therefore great :
Else were it little worth :

PRINCESS.   The Earl's modesty
All Gascony redeems, else might we claim him
English : But I doubt me he's French at heart.
What say you my good lord ?

EARL. I am old, fair lady, but were I young
I would be England's; for the same reason
Men wish for Heav'n, because there angels dwell.

PRINCESS. Ah, flatterer, too young by half.

PRINCE. My lord, these dogs are of a noble race.

EARL. Alans, your Grace, of power to pull down
Stag, boar, or wolf, which I have heard you love
To hunt; and with these casts of falcons, brought
In earnest of my service.   Please it you
To honour me by their acceptance.

PRINCE.   I
Take them thankfully.   Yes I love the chace;
After hard ride the felon wolf to slay,
Or see the arm'd boar rush upon the spear,
His hot breath on your face, straining to reach
With foaming rage and ivory tusk your life:
'Tis all the joy of war without its pains.
So then our young friend is to leave us, Earl?

EARL. With your highness' leave:

PRINCE.   Well, you'll find your son
Versed in all accomplishments that may
Be learn'd in a noble house: 'Tis true,
'Tis time he won his spurs.

EARL.   Albeit my son,
Rear'd in the very school of chivalry
I will pledge him perfect.

PRINCESS. But me it grieves to lose so true a knight;
Dear Gaston, I know him one will never
Shame his tutelage.

GAS.   Dear and honour'd lady,
Let me offer on my knee the homage—
The deep gratitude of a still young heart,
Not only for my princely entertainment,
(For which to 's Highness my great thanks are due)
But for such love as guardian angels spread
O'er their appointed charge.   Noble Lady,
For this presence my wrung heart is too full,
And all the boy is rising to my throat,
To shame these new-donn'd arms.   But may the time,
O may the time arrive when this weak arm
Can be of service to so dear a mistress,
Hallowing my knightly sword, and try me
To the utterance.

PRINCESS.   Go now, good Gaston,
Or I too shall melt; stay—this chain—wear it
For my sake, wherever honour calls you;
Ever in the front rank.

GAS.   O! to the death!
(*To the* PRINCE) Your highness' leave?

PRINCE.   God bless thee; go and wait
On the Castle terrace, till your father
Is ready for departure; we have yet

Some matters to discourse of.   [*Exit* GASTON.

                              A fair youth,

My lord earl, and a noble ; wants iron.

   EARL. 'Twill come, your Grace, by hammering ; this
    realm

Doth seldom want for blows.

   PRINCE.   You say most true,

There seems to be no end of these sad wars,

And my heart bleeds for the poor towns, that live

In an ebb and flow of blood and pillage :

One day held by the French ; the next by us.

And who in the heat of conquest can control

The madded soldiery ? while their leaders,

Deeming the citizens not true to them,

Restrain them not, but share the pollute spoil :

Poor wretched burghers, if they dare resist

They find no mercy ; if helpless they yield ;

By the next conqueror they're traitors deem'd :

And so God's image strews this woful earth,

And the whole land is soak'd with brother's blood.

Are they not men, and women, (poor women !)

And children that we slay ?   O piteous thought !

A sad world—a sad world and a weary ;

'Tis past our power to mend.   Please you, this way.

                              [*Exeunt.*

SCENE 2.—*The Castle Terrace.*

GASTON *alone.*

Love!

Mere folly! a delusion of the sense!
Of what avail is free will if fetter'd
By this all alike compelling power?
Can we not resist, defy this thraldom?
Vain all resistance, we but strike the air:
But for this tyranny how great were man:
But for this inward tyrant he were free:
Yet is it not a chain of love that binds
The lowest to the highest, the greatest
Virtues to the basest crimes, heav'n to earth?
Alas, alas! is there no way to 'scape?
O Isabel, Isabel, Isabel!
And see,—as answering to my invocation,
Where she enhaloed in her beauty comes:
Better absent,—for then I think—and joy;
When present,—realise despair! down heart.—

Enter ISABEL.

ISA. O dear Gaston: They told me you were here,
And I came to seek you: you look so sad:
My poor boy what is it? *(she kisses him).*

GAS. I must speak and feign : (*aside*).
Isabel I lack sympathy, I've none
To lean upon ; my father loves his son ;
But he's stern and has little time for aught
Beyond his state affairs ; then my brother
Once lov'd me, but is chang'd.

    ISA.   And your sister ?

    GAS. O would to God, you were !

    ISA. Am I not ? my affection do you doubt ?
From childhood have we not each other lov'd ?
Each other's joys and sorrows we have shared ;
And now you leave us is your trust all gone ?
Do I not love you still ?

    GAS.   This is torment
Impossible to bear :— Listen to me :
Isabel you're above the common arts
Of women, and your clear soul is guiltless
Of all thought of deceit ; and yet 'tis strange !
Intuitive perception is the gift
Of woman ; can it be,—this affection—
Of which you speak—is all has grown with you,
And all you deem, I feel ? that deepening blush !
I see the scales are falling from your eyes ;
They have long fall'n from mine : O Isabel !
Not as a brother do I love you now :
And you,—O do not answer suddenly,

If 'tis to blast my dear expectancy.—

O those tears——

Let me a little longer yet remain

In this suspense,—this dream,—this hope that yet;

If you cannot repeat,—as now you said,

" Do I not love you still ; " I still may cling

A little longer to the hope, that yet

'Twill be.

    Isa.   O grief!

    Gas.   Speak not dear Isabel ;

But hear me.   How long I've lov'd I know not :

I only know 't has so grown with my life,

That not to love you now, were not to live.

No fearful mariner, cast forth by night

Upon the storm-lash'd waves on fragment wreck,

E'er watch'd for the first roseate streaks of dawn

As I have watch'd to catch from your dear face

The first faint dawn of love.—*It never came !*

O I have waited—waited through pain'd years :

It never came ! As girl, I've seen with grief

Your maiden blush bless other happy hearts

With feeling kindred to the love I sought ;

And pensive I have seen you stand,—at times

When other's praise has reach'd your ear : Ah me !

No praise of mine has ever made you blush ;

No love of mine has ever caus'd you thought :

And then you grew to womanhood ; while I—
You thought me still a boy :—but my love grew
To adoration.   And when you've kiss'd me,
As you will do no more ; a poison sweet
Was pour'd through all my blood.   How came it—
    you—
You saw it not.   I've felt the earth whirl round
While I forc'd back the torrent to my heart
That else had master'd me.—And by your side,
When masques and plays and deeds of arms in list
With buoyant joy you've watch'd, I saw them not ;
I saw but you,—nothing I saw but you.
My father half monk deems me and half coward,
That I lead not his banner 'gainst our foes ;
O Isabel, with ecstasy I'd rush
Bare breasted 'gainst ten thousand spears to win—
If but to win from you one look of love,
And die content !

    ISA.   Dear Gaston, I have borne
Small sorrows and imaginary woes,
But this the first great grief my heart has wrung :
O why was I so blind ? and yet,—O no—
I ever thought your love for me the same
As mine for you, that of a brother dear :
Else might this have been—

    GAS.   No—oh no ! oh no !

Isa. Say not so; even now if you would rouse
Your dormant spirits and shake off this thrall,
And striving for the high prize of ambition
Shine forth among the chivalry of France;
Then with achiev'd success and glory crown'd
You'd thank me that I thwart this boyish love,
Which cannot last,—

Gas.   Not last? O Isabel,
Either you speak not from your heart—or you—
O precious hope—have never lov'd: That sigh!
O Isabel have pity, now you know—
All—all my misery. Search, if perchance
You cannot find some feeling which you've thought
Fraternal,—but which may if cherish'd warm
To a dearer name; for sure that treasure of the heart
Is not irrevocably lost to me.
O have mercy.

Isa.   It is impossible!

Gas. No, say not so: O drive me not distract:
For your own sake—your safety—say not so.

Isa. How? a threat! Gaston 'tis unkind from you.

Gas. I! wither may my tongue within my mouth
Ere utter aught to you but fearful love,
Deep, fearful love. Listen to me; the Earl
Has this alliance settled with your father:
I begg'd for time because I would not owe

To power what I could not gain from love :
Without the heart the hand is little worth.

Isa. Dear Gaston, this is your generous self.
Some one comes.

Gas.   Is there no hope ? do you love—
Do you love another ?

Isa. Alas ! alas !

Gas.   Grant me strength !

Enter the Princess.

Princess. Gaston, your father waits you.
What ! confusion,—blushes,—my poor children !
O then I see the cocatrice is hatch'd.

Marshall (within). To horse, to horse ! Trumpets
        sound !
My lord Gaston to the Earl's banner :
Knights to the van ! trumpets sound !
Forward !   *(flourish.)*

  Gas. Farewell, dear, dear Isabel ; but this once ;

                                  (kissss her.)
Forgive me honoured lady, God in Heaven
Bless you. Farewell. *(Kneels and kisses the Princess'
                        hand and exit.)*

  Princess. If your father favour it my child,
It may be well ; for 'tis the poor alone,
Whose hearts of free love have the privilege :

Our hearts, dear Isabel, are not our own ;
Warp'd from their right bias by policy
Or gold ; aye—though they break.　　　　*[Exit.*

　　Isa.　　　　　　　　Beside the mark
She aims.　Alas, poor Gaston, he loves me :
As one restor'd to sight sees nothing clear,
This light breaks on me and my mind is daz'd ;
How sunk his pleading tones into my soul,
As now their echo draws the streaming tears
From my grief-blinded eyes : so the lightning
Cleaving the thunder-cloud brings down the rain :
He is not my brother—yet I love him—
Dearly love him, though no longer brother.
How ! what does this mean ? did I not know this
And still went loving on, deceiving self ;
Gilding the steel and dreaming it was gold
Until it pierc'd me ? now my eyes unfilm,
Leaving my heart full fill'd with a great love
For one who is a stranger ; and my hand
Already pledg'd :—how different their love !
For Evain with his manly bearing took
All suddenly my maiden fancy captive ;
And now he takes my love as 'twere his due,
And holds my jewel with as light a grasp
As the merlin on his glove ; while Gaston
Would give the world's wealth for one ray from it
And die to win it :—yes—how different :　　*[Exeunt.*

SCENE 3.—*Camp before Malvoisin.*

DUKE OF ANJOU, EARL OF FOIX *and Suites.*

ANJ. Look to 't my lord ; I have a pow'r on foot
Would like nought better than to overrun
Your country, wealthy with so long a rest.
Peace gain'd by double dealing !

FOIX.   Be just, your Grace,
Be just.   If my poor country I have kept
Unscath'd although surrounded by unfriends,
May I not some honour rather challenge,
And from a son of France, of whom I hold
My earldom, thanks?   Shall I unaided brave
The power of England—I—a simple earl ?
And if I did, would France uphold me ?—No !

ANJ. My lord we ask it not, but is it right
That you should furnish men and knights to war
Against us ? men are rais'd in Foix and Bearn
To man the forts for England : when I lead
My forces against theirs it is to fight
Frenchmen ! French slay French, giving to England
A double gain.

FOIX.   In these unruly times
Men seek for service where they reap best pay :
All leaders employ these mercenaries
That roam the realm for hire.

ANJ.   Sooth, I grant ye—

When they're common men : but when your kinsmen

Lead them ? what is this but levying war

Against your liege lord ?

FOIX.   Whom do you accuse ?

ANJ. To leave those of lesser note, your cousin,

Sir Ernalton of Bearn, holds out the fort

Of Lourdes against the power of France.

FOIX.   'Tis true.

But Bearn is free, and homage owes to none

But Foix : Sir Ernalton is no vassal

Of France, although my kinsman.

ANJ.   Are you not ?

FOIX. No, not for Bearn ; and if the knights of

   Bearn

I call upon to serve on either side

At the command of France, what is it less

Than to make Bearn a fief of France ?

ANJ.   A subterfuge !

FOIX. Your Grace is privileged in speech.

ANJ.   Well, well,

Earl you are warn'd ; and as I know I speak

To one of wisdom tried, remember yet

That this same Prince, this duke of Aquitaine,

Is but a stranger, of the crown of France

Himself a vassal.   Your sagacity

May tell you that in course of time this realm

Will not submit a foreign foe to hold

Within its borders ; and that ere long—

    Foix.   Aye

This well may be, but never in our day :

The peers of France are now too jealous far,

Each of the other,—to unite their bands

Against intruders.   Is not all the realm

Sore lacerated by their civil jars ?

Peer against peer, and chief opposed to chief ?

And under cover of this general strife

Is every peaceful hamlet overrun

By captains of Companions ; who while knights

And barons on these quarrels are away,

Seize on their strongholds, and with fire and sword

Harry the fair fields, sack the villages,

And hold to ransom the poor peasantry.

    Anj. This should not be : but while it is,—as yet

I see no sign it will be otherwise,

We must submit to see our soil defaced

By the proud warlike tramp of England's host.

Oh that we had a king ! the nation then

Would with one universal shout arise,

And each man feel with indignation fierce,

That every foreign footstep on the soil

Of France, trod on his mother's bosom :—Then

With overwhelming torrent energy
Cast forth th' invader, and redeem the shame
Of Cressy and Poitiers, reconsecrate
Our desecrated land, and be indeed
A kingdom.

    Foix.   Amen, amen.

    Anj.   Is't from your heart?

    Foix.   It is.

    Anj. We will speak more of this.   O come the day
And France be France from Calais to Bordeaux;
Until no man remain, will dare to breathe
He ever favour'd England.   Grant it Heaven!

                                      ᐟ [*Exeunt.*

———o———

SCENE 4.—*Ortaise.*   *The Hostelry of the Moon.*

RAYMONET DE L'EPÉE, ARNULPH, BASIL, *Host,*
Retainers of FOIX *and* ARMAGNAC, *Troopers of Free*
Lances, Peasants of Foix and Bearn.

    Ray. Wine, host! wine!   D'Armagnac?
I say he was sham'd.

    Bas.   Varlet, thou liest!
Shame and my master were ne'er on one side
The hedge.

RAY.   I care not on which side the hedge
Thy master rides, but sure I am 'tis not
On the same side with his foes.   Hear me, knave;
And if thou say'st not that my tale is sooth,
By good St. James I'll make thee eat thy words,
Or try the temper of my curtal axe
Upon thy crown.

HOST.   'Ware brawling in Ortaise!

RAY. Mind thy tally, host; and bring more wine:
Hear me companions.   Did not th' Earl of Foix,
When d'Armagnac defied him in Cassères,
Which with two hundred men at arms he held,
Did not the Earl in scorn build up the gates,
And shut them in like rats? Did he not swear
No man of them should pass those gates alive?
Aye, and he kept his word.   And when they sued
For mercy, the good Earl wanted not blood,
But ransom; yet how?—not to break his oath,
He ordered them a hole make in the wall,
And issue one by one as prisoners;
And so they did.   I laugh yet at the thought:
I saw the proud lords d'Albret and d'Armagnac
Upon knees creeping with dishonoured crests
Through a dusty hole i' the wall; he not shamed?
And ransom paid two hundred thousand francs!

BAS. Pay or not pay, he was not sham'd; thou liest!

RAY.   (*Strikes him down with his battle-axe.*)
Who lies now? and low? I've kept my word!

ARN. D'Armagnac to the rescue! I'll not see
A comrade struck down in my lord's defence,
And not strike in! A d'Armagnac! Come on!

RAY. A Gaston! A Foix; down with the knaves!

(*General uproar.*)

Enter SIR MAULÉON *and* AIMERY.

MAU. Ho! keep the peace, ye knaves.   Free blades
to me,
Part these mad woodsmen: down with their axes:

(*The Free Companions rush between the
combatants and separate them.*)

If some of ye are not so fortunate
As to be kill'd, ye'll hardly 'scape shaving
By the Earl's provost, without a razor:
Ye know if this brawl came to the Earl's ears,
Your heads ere morn were playthings for the wolves.

BAS. Good Captain, I am slain—some help—I die!

MAU. Be thankful: thou'lt 'scape heading:
Who rose the fray?

BAS.   Impugning my lord's honour!—

RAY. True, Sir Mauléon, so he gave me the lie;
And so I smote him: then both parties join'd.

MAU. Thou hadst some cause to strike; the lie given
Is a fair cause of quarrel: But for thee,

Thou idiot! is it in thine indentures
To be the keeper of thy master's honour?
If 'twere worse than 'tis, it would nought mend
In such unworthy keeping. Knight's honour,
Like woman's chastity, when it has fall'n
Of brawls in hostels to become the theme,
Has lost its bloom and threadbare is indeed.
We are soldiers: take an old man's advice,
Since I was twenty, I am now threescore,
I have been a captain of Companions,
And have served in every nation's wars;
And in these homicidal times should scarce
Have pass'd my youth, if I had ruffled it
With every long sword with a tongue to match
That did not think my chief immaculate:
'Tis for fighting ye are paid: let your lords
Defend themselves their honour; little they have,
And ye have none.

ARN.   Hold there, Sir Mauléon.
'Tis not within your homily I trow,
That every man may not defend his own;
And you have slander'd us collectively:
We are an honourable profession.

MAU. Good! thou man of honour! thine argument?

ARN. The verdict of the world.

MAU.   'Gainst evidence:

Art thou not asham'd, for thou'st seen service,
To talk of soldier's honour? give the lie
To thine own throat? are ye not a proverb?
I grant ye patience and fidelity,
If not too sorely tempted, and courage;
Collective honour?   Collective devils!
Ye know the crimes yourselves commit in war
To hear of in cold blood would make your nerves
To crisp with horror.   Could I not tell ye
Deeds of outrage, murder, oft they haunt me
In the dead of night, which your profession
Honourable perpetrate? which bathe ye
In an ocean Stygian of dishonour!
To your quarters ere this fray get wind,
Or we may not screen ye—away!

                [*Exeunt* SIR MAULÉON *and* AIMERY.

ARN.   For all that,
An' it were not for thy grey hair and rank,
Thou should'st not have carried it so easily:
Here, empty the flagon and be friends all;
And damn honour.   [*Exeunt.*

SCENE 5.—*Hall in the Castle of Ortaise. Walls hung with armour and weapons, Men-at-arms in attendance.*

Enter THE EARL, GASTON, SIR ERNALTON OF BEARN, BASTOT DE MAULÉON, SIR JOHN FROISSART, *Knights and Squires, Huntsmen and Falconers.*

EARL. By St. Hubert, Gaston, a glorious flight;
Where gat ye your falcons? a noble cast.

GAS. Icelanders, my lord: from a gipsey gang
I purchased them.

EARL.   They soar'd a higher pitch
Than my best passage hawks; but they're wild,
And do not "wait on" steadily.

GAS.   My lord,
They were flown "at hack" till within this month:
I tried them but to see if they were fit
To offer my dear father.

EARL.   A good lad:
I'll take thy gift the rather that these knaves
Say not thou soar'st above thy father's pitch.

FROI. The wind-warp'd multitude is credulous.

EARL. Gaston, when thou art lord of these domains
Watch thou the wind; guide it,—or fix the vane.

GAS. God grant me a long tutelage.   But now
I would of my dear father crave a boon,

To be a short time absent in Navarre
To see my mother; if it please you.

    EARL.   Ha!
To what end would you go? Josselin! I say!

Enter JOSSELIN.

That cast of kestril kites that miss'd their swoop,
Straight wring their necks and cast them to the dogs,
And put their varvels on these silver skins
Of Gaston's.

    JOS.   Does your lordship mean the pair
Received from the Duke of Anjou?

    EARL.   I do!

    JOS. O my lord, they'll mend; I had as lief kill
My child.   (*The* EARL *looks at him. Exit* JOSSELIN.)

    EARL. Gaston, what want you in Navarre?

    GAS. Dear my lord, I've said 'tis but to offer
My love and duty to my mother,
Whom I've not seen for long and long to see
With yearning heart.

    EARL.   Son, it is natural;
Nor would I wish to fray the holy tie
That binds you to her: of our estrangement
Her brother was the cause, who once obtained
Large sums of money that were due to me;
He then induced your mother to remain

With him, and then forsooth put forth the plea
It was her dowry, which he would not yield.
From fear of him at first she stayed,
Then dread of my just wrath widen'd the breach
Irreparably : Go, you have my leave ;
I cannot on this subject speak with calm.

 GAS. Can I no message?

 EARL.   None! [*Exit* EARL.

 GAS.   My poor father!

I cannot realise this grief, and yet
I may the sorrow partly understand
Of being wife forsaken, if it be
In aught like a first love without return ;
For that too bitterly I feel : How worse
It must be, after dreams of mutual love
Blessing the progress of the happy years,
To wake to hate : And all for what? gold! that!
I would I had some power to heal this breach :
Alas, too late, too late !

     Re-enter the EARL.

     How stern he looks:
How deeply have I mov'd him, if 'tis this.

 ERN. May it please you?—

 EARL.   It would please me better
Had I friends about me that I could trust.
What would you ?

ERN.   I came Sir at your summons,
And for three idle days have feasted here;
Unto my charge I ask now to return,
Tendering for your hospitality
My poor thanks and duty.

EARL.   Duty, cousin?
Yes, 'tis of that I'd speak: it was for that
I crav'd your presence; I marvel that you came:
Can you teach me cousin, for you're learned,
The casuistry by which a man can serve
Two masters? in what way you reconcile
Your present service with the Prince of Wales,
With your duty to your humble kinsman
Though liege lord, the Earl of Foix? what say you?

ERN. 'T has ever been the custom of good knights
To raise their fame by val'rous deeds of arms;
Study the art of war in any school:
Your country is at peace: were 't otherwise,
Mine and my vassals' services were yours,
From whom I hold my seignories, before
The Prince of Wales, whom I will leave if you
Require my sword.

EARL.   'Tis not always with sword
A knight can serve his lord. Sir Ernalton,
You've brought me into peril which I brook not;
But for th' entreaties of myself and friends,

The Duke of Anjou had o'errun my lands,
And done me deadly scathe : because forsooth
You are my cousin, and hold Lourdes castle
For the Prince, against him : he charges me
That I sustain you, for you are of Bearn.
Not for your sake will I hold enmity
With prince so great, a prince the heir of France.
'Tis not enough you quit the English side ;
But at your worst peril I command ye,
By the faith and homage that you owe us,
That you deliver up the garrison
Of Lourdes and its castle into my hands.

    Enn. My lord, it grieves me that your courtesy
Should have no other aim : This your command
Between two equal perils places me :
Know you not? if not—I tell you now,
I've sworn an oath against all men to keep
This castle for the King of England.
'Tis true, I am a poor knight of your blood
And country, and therefore owe you fealty ;
And in danger stand of your displeasure
If I disobey : but if I comply,
I am false to a sacred trust, forsworn,
Dishonour'd ! and that I will never be.

    Earl. Ha ! beware !

    Ern.   Sir, I will not deliver it :

I now hold it of the Prince for England :
To him I'm pledg'd : do with me as you please,
For to no other living man but him
Will I deliver it.

 EARL.   Say'st thou ?

 ERN.   My lord,
I've said !

 EARL.   Ha ! vassal, say'st thou so ?
Now by my head thou hast not spoke for nought.
Death ! (*The Earl in ungovernable rage stabs him, he*
         falls supported by Gaston.)

 ERN. St. Mary ! help ! ah, sir,—this was unkind !
To send for me in peace, and 'gainst all faith
To slay me ! Gaston, your arm ; may my blood,
This blood which now stains you, prove no omen
Of judgment for this deed—on you—or him,—
My dear lord whom in death I love and honour.
        (*He is carried out.*)

 FROI. My lord, I fear this cruelty when known
In princes' courts will blacken your good name ;
Beneath his tent the Arab spares his foe ;
But Christians slay their brothers with home-bread
Upon their lips. All men must condemn it,
History blazon it to future times :
Now—no man trust your safeguard.

 EARL.   I gave none !

Drivelling dotard !   I crave your pardon,

You move me past endure.   To be defied !

Do you not know all history one lie

Composed of gossip, hearsay, common fame ?

And were it true ? it cannot hurt the dead :

To be brav'd !   Cruelty ? is't not better

To fall thus by hand of knight than suffer

By the headsman ? for such was his desert.

The deed irks me not.   Stay, call Sir Aimery.

Enter Sir Aimery.

Have you your troops at hand, the number full ?

How many do you muster ?

Aim.   Two hundred.

Earl. No more ? and you Sir Mauléon ?

Mau.   Fourscore.

Earl. 'Tis little for attacking Lourdes.

Aim.   Besides

'Tis said Sir Ernalton before he left

His brother swore to die in its defence

If he return'd not; and further charg'd him

No orders to obey, even from him,

To render it: and this his brother swore;

T' attack it then were useless, so prepar'd.

Earl. A staunch villain : he has gone beyond us :

Would that we had more such on our side.

[*Exeunt.*

ACT II.

SCENE 1.—*The Mews.*

JOSSELIN *the Falconer*, HALBERT *his man.*

Jos. I cannot do it! my beautiful falcons! O Ralph, Ralph, when you were six furlongs high, free, free! why did you not escape? And there you sit poor innocents, unconscious of your doom.

Hal. Never whine for a bird: knights and squires have no better fate.

Jos. O but they love me, and are so gentle. Poor Sultan! Halbert, 'tis a breach of confidence; creatures that will leave their free skies, and come to your hand —and to kill them?

Hal. Well, don't; send them away, you may trust me.

Jos. Tho' I could trust your love—your fear I could not; if the Earl question'd you, you dare not deceive him, nor could you, if you would. O Ralph, Sultan! See their deep brown eyes; they almost speak; and I must—kill you;—I cannot, yet the Earl must be

T

obeyed.   He stabb'd the knight—what mercy for a
falconer? and another would give them more pain.
Halbert, can you imagine why men take such pleasure
in killing? pass for wars—but knights running courses
with spears, and jousting with sword and battle-axe,
to no end but to kill each other—and all in pure
friendship: my poor falcons!

HAL. Why should they not kill each other?   I think
of turning man-at-arms myself: if I kill I get money;
if I'm kill'd, I'm provided for.

JOS. Ah, Halbert, better to lead a quiet life, and fly
your hawks where you list.   We are the true masters;
maintain'd at ease.   O Ralph, Ralph, Ralph!

HAL. Ay, ay! witness your present trouble: Master
Josselin you're a slave; I would be free, at no man's
beck.   As for life,—it's a struggle into it,—a struggle
through it,—and a struggle out of it.

JOS. Well, take off their jesses and bells: what
swoops I have seen them make! how their wings
flash'd! come, I must do 't in the dark; I can't bear
their eyes on me.

(*As he is going out, enter* EVAIN.)

EVA. Hallo, Josselin, whither wend ye?

JOS. Not far, my young lord, yet a sad heart makes
A long journey.

EVA.   A truce to your riddles.

Jos. Sir, the Earl your father has order'd me
These falcons—once his favourites to kill.

Eva. The devil! and why?

Jos.   Why? they were out-soar'd
By a new cast of my young lord Gaston's;
There they stand; I like not these Icelanders
White feather'd.   Are not these more beautiful?

Eva. And these you are to kill? sure my father
Could not mean it Josselin; give them to me.

Jos. Your father seldom says what he means not;
My life would not be safe.

Eva.   I will have them.

(*He snatches up a lure, and shouting whoop, who-hoop,
the falcons leave the cadge, and alight on his
shoulders.*)

Jos. Desist my lord, you've taken them by force.

Eva. Rather by their good will, but mean to keep
them.

Jos. I must tell the Earl.

Eva.   Dare, or even dare
To say 't again, I'll drive my dirk through you.

[*Exit with falcons.*

Hal. That's what I call Jupiter coming down
And making all square—I saw 't at a masque.

Jos. I fear me some danger will come of it.

Hal. Yes, but not whence you think; my master

you are ; but not a master wit.   My small wit tells me
you are sav'd the pain of killing your hawks, and you
have an answer for the Earl should he discover it,
which is not likely.

Jos. St. Hubert grant it.

Hal. But beware master Evain, he's no tiercel gentil
and unless soon cop'd will do mischief.

———o———

SCENE 2.—*Outside the Castle.*

Evain, *alone.*

So, master falconer, your hawks are lur'd ;
Yet do I not intend that they should live ;
But only that you know not they are dead :
For I would not without necessity
Be cruel.   Certes, his life were little worth
Knew but the Earl he had been disobey'd ;
But Josselin believing them alive
Is in my power, and so becomes my thrall.
Friends I must have, whether of love or fear,
To raise the bastard, if it may be so,
Ay, over his more noble brother's head.
And here he comes.   On, angel-borrow'd mask ;
Be all brother, till time's seal—occasion
Shatter the visor, and bring the issue.

Enter GASTON.

Ah, my dear, dear brother, with what great joy
I see you, be this embrace my witness.
How 'scap'd you from the giant in black mail
Who holds his castle by the river Lys?
And yet methinks, 'twere easier to scale
His walls, than break the stronger silken cords
That bind the heart.

GAS.   My father thought 'twas time
That I should leave such training, and take part
In the rough turmoil of this jarring world;
The Prince conseuted.   Believe me, brother,
Under the brightest corslet in all France
Breathes not a nobler spirit than there lives
Under that sombre mail, which seems to veil
The glory of the sun of Chivalry.

EVA. Whose dazzling rays with the more moonlike
    beams
From the Princess' eyes have turn'd you English;
Unless the light of Isabel's fair eyes
Has lur'd you back again.

GAS.   Why jest you thus?
'Tis true the Princess' true knight I am sworn,
And shall not prove a recreant.   I love her
As a mother.

Eva. May be ; but we who've been
More roughly nurtur'd believe not such love ;
I have a mother and I love her well,
Albeit she brought me not into the world
According to the canon : but preserve me
From any other pretty woman's love
Behind so frail a curtain : a device
Of Satan.   I'm no monk, tho' if all's true
They are most monks who are least monks.
When I love, I strike hands before the world.   No, no ;
Mother's love in a stranger is a mere
Drifting into sin ; sinning filially.

Gas. You were ever a scoffer, brother mine.

Eva. Only 'gainst those who use so fair a name,
So holy, to cover so foul a fault.

Gas. (*aside*) To whom can I unfold my deepest
grief ?
His nature my heart repels—'tis seeming.

Eva. You have not answer'd to the second count,
My Gaston ; the fair Isabel, doubtless,
You love as a sister ?

Gas. (*aside*) No, I cannot
Open my tense heart to his assur'd scorn.
Dear brother, I am too sad for anger,
Or such words might make a severance
Between our loves which ever have been one.

Eva. Hold they by so slight a tie? A light word,
A minute's breath, to snap the chain of years.
Methought love was more lasting : you are chang'd.

   Gas. Chang'd, Evain? well now you say 't, I am
     chang'd,
But not to you. (*aside*) I would I could trust him
     more.

    Eva. (*aside*) I see his heart as though his breast
     were glass.
Is 't only your regret to leave behind
The lily fair of Tarbes? or has aught marr'd
Your peace, safety? my arm and sword are yours :
My head—alas there are no brains in it
Worth aught to help your counsels with their aid.

   Gas. Thanks brother, no troubles threat me from
     without,
But within I've somewhat to make thoughtful
One of riper years ; 'tis but yesterday,
No cares I had but dress, and paying court
To bright eyed beauty ; a pleasant service
For pliant boyhood, or for buoyant youth.
To-day, as metal forc'd into the mould
Anneal'd for service, my all of bright youth
Is crush'd into the man, and I must think
And act. Well, I confess I did not quit
The lovely vale of Tarbes ungrieved—that vale,

Through which the river Lys its limpid stream
Clear as a fountain pours : full twelve feet deep
The fish you see as floating in the air ;
And all around the vine and tree-clad hills
Embosom the fair town ; while far above
The Pyrenean hills upjet their peaks,
And pink their snows against the morning sun.
The maids of Tarbes I sometime thought were fair,
Until the Lady Isabel appeared ;
Then faded all their charms as stars at dawn,
And all men worshipped her.   But he on whom
The conscious glory of her beauty shines
Will be most blest.

  EVA.   Is he not known ?

  GAS.   Oh no !

And still the pangs of the three goddesses
Lie deep and calm in each devoted heart
That lives upon her looks and magnifies
Each smile, deeming the prize his own. *[Exit.*

  EVA. Mine is the prize good brother, an earnest
Of more to come, which you think yours : and yet
I care not for a thing so valueless
As woman's love.   Trust that ! the devotion
Of a true woman is a thing so rare,
'Tis wonder'd at an 'twere a prodigy,
Which it would not be were it general.

Woman loves to be lov'd ; her love is self ;
And who first worships that, secures her love,
The reflex lightness of a shallow heart.
O 'tis a bitter mockery ! 'tis born
Of heart ache, pangs, and gifts and sufferings ;
'Tis fostered by devotion, only less
Than what man pays his God ; matured by all
The highest, truest feelings of man's heart ;
Yet 'tis hollow at the core. No sooner
Smiles on the beauteous tree the ardent sun,
Or threats the storm, it falls and crushes him !
Trust woman's love ! The poor deluded fool
Who on his idol has lavish'd all his soul,
Scarce has he given his body to the soil
To fatten cabbages, or leeks or docks,
Ere she will eat a salad from his grave,
Her hollow love given to another mate :
And so from fool to fool !
No, let Isabel love me—bring with her
All her large inheritance ; I'll meet her
With a comprehensive love, involving
Both her and hers ; leaving me free as air.

———o———

SCENE 3.—*Navarre. An Apartment.*

The DUKE, *alone.*

Why hesitate? It is not that I fear
To take his life—but the means? for the wrong
Done to a dear sister, his best blood shed
Were all too little ; thus to cast her off, —
In her chaste home to see strangers revel :
I am old now else he dar'd not do it :
But though swordless, I am not weaponless
If my intent hold good.   A poisoner ?
It sounds not well ; my better nature shrinks—
Shudders to grasp this weapon of the weak :
Say he escape, and I sit tamely down
Under this flagrant shame, pining my heart
With unappeased revenge ; Gaston his son
Is next cast off, and all his heritage
Devised to his bastards.   This must not be :
Restor'd shall be his mother to her rights,
Gaston shall be Earl.   Him that I would slay
Openly with the sword, being young and strong ;
Being old and weak I hold it equal justice
To slay by policy.

SCENE 4.—*A Room in the Palace.*

COUNTESS OF FOIX. GASTON *in travelling dress.*

COUN. And must you go so soon, my dear, dear
    child?
Again I lose you: my heart misgives me
That I may never, never see you more.
    GAS. O but you shall, and that ere long. You
    know
Dear mother, now I've left the Prince's court
I am more free to follow my own will;
And that will lead me to my mother's heart.
    COUN. Yet I cannot cast off from me this dread.
What would you, Gaston? I see some purpose
In your features strive; speak, your mother hears.
    GAS. Dear my mother, if my love gives me right
So far to trespass, I would on my knees
Entreat your fair return; for my father
Is noble and generous, and would hail
Your vouchsaf'd return with joy.
    COUN.   Said he so?
Boy, you little know your father; reverence
Blinds you: had you but seen him in his ire
As I have; friend and foe alike go down

Before the blinded storm : for when incens'd
He knows no mercy.

   GAS.   Mother, I have :

Can I forget ? tis not a week—I saw
That brave knight Sir Ernalton ;—he refused
To break his faith pledg'd to the Prince of Wales,
When summon'd by my father to give up
Of Lourdes the castle to the King of France.
He was his cousin, but he stabb'd him there.

   COUN. O piteous tale ! and is the good knight slain ?

   GAS. Or ere the words had pass'd his lips his blood
Flew over me : my father slew a man ;
I judge him not ; but not in woman's heart
Should apprehension dwell : to her alone
His iron spirit bends that bows to none
On earth : O mother if—

   COUN.   Enough my son.

Time was your father lov'd me ; proud I was,
My pride is fall'n, of such a noble mate.
But now, that love once mine—all gone—or giv'n
To others. Have you not brothers, Gaston,
Brothers,—think awhile, and not my children ?
And can you urge me to return ? And yet
Knowing your coming hither, had he sent
One loving word to his forsaken wife,
I know not if I should have had the power

To remain.   Dear son, you know he did not :
Nor would I by intrusion peril you ;
Had I been wish'd, the Earl by you had sent
His plain command,—he's wont to be obeyed ;
You cannot say he did.

GAS.   Mother, alas,
He spake not of it.   Farewell, dear mother :
I go to take leave of the Duke, and then
To horse ;—kiss me mother, and your blessing.

COUN. No, come to me again before you go ;
I would part with my child more privately,
I would not break down here ; my dear, dear child,
Should I not see you more !   Gaston, you'll come ?

GAS. Mother dear, I will.   [*Exeunt.*

———o———

SCENE 5.—*The Same.*

THE DUKE OF NAVARRE, GASTON.

GAS. Noble sir, I would crave your leave.
DUKE.   You're sad.
GAS. Marvel not I'm sad, I lose a mother.
DUKE. Do you love your mother ?

GAS. Do I love my mother?

DUKE. Nephew I grieve for you, but cannot trust
My tongue to name the Earl, of whom to speak
Without honour before his son, would not
Be generous, even from the brother
Of his discarded mother. So, no more.
If there be aught that I can serve you in,
My revenues you may command, and aid
If need be to secure your heritage,
Or from aggression to protect your rights.

GAS. My lord, of this world's goods I have enough,
And gold, the great fiend, I ever hated
Except for necessary use.

DUKE.   And yet
'Tis only by its means we can acquire
Broad lands and seignories, earldoms and realms.

GAS. For these I care not : as a boy I've watch'd
Two beetles fighting for a ball of soil,
A perfect sphere, that with their struggles roll'd
Like fortune's wheel ; now one was up ; now down ;
Each from the top the other hurls, till one,
Achieves by striving hard the rolling dirt.
Such are man's struggles for pre-eminence
Upon this earth : and when the height is gain'd
Of his ambition, as worthless is the prize.

DUKE. Youth turn'd philosopher ! your comparison

Is foul as foolish. When your hair's dark woof
'Is warp'd with silver, such visionary
Notions you'll abjure. No, 'tis not for lands,
No, nor for gold and silver that men strive ;
These but a worthless scarabean prize.
'Tis power, Gaston : mark me, 'tis power,
Power to sway the destinies of men,
Whether the sphere a province, town or realm ;
God-like power, the true prize of ambition !
Power to guide kingdoms and to sway the world,
Unswayed by none.

  Gas.   O yes, by One.

  Duke.   Not man !

Well for the world this passion's rare in youth :
But one Alexander was, for whose vast
Ambition scarce sufficed this entire earth.
Well, 'twill come, fair nephew ; 'twill come with years.

  Gas. It may, but now youth's troubles may suffice.

  Duke. For youth's troubles even an old man may feel.
Tell me, how fares your suit with Isabel,
The young sister of d'Armagnac's proud Earl ?

  Gas. Alas, my lord, I cannot win her love :
She hears my pleadings with an unmov'd brow ;
Yet has my father settled it must be ;
And I may have her person with her hate ;
Rather her love, and she a cloister'd nun !

DUKE. Upon this mystery 'tis not for age
To argue with the fiery blood of youth,
Test th' impalpable by hard experience,
Or reason with the irrational.   But what?
Touch a man's passion, or of heart or head,
You hear no more of his philosophy!
Ambition the stoic moves not, nor gold;
Yet to obtain the baseless boon of love
He'd kneel to man or fiend.

GAS.   If man could help,
I'd kneel to him until my hair grew grey;
But no infernal force can influence love;
God-like that is; such is not always power.

DUKE. You remind me of my youth:
I fain would help you.

GAS.   That you had the means!

DUKE. Perhaps I have, and might.

GAS.   How? what mean you?

DUKE. Listen; you may have heard I've been long
    time
A student of the natural sciences;
And the wonders I have prov'd, the vulgar
Would fain set down as miracles, such as
The transmutation of the baser metals
Into gold; the fire's generation
From cold salts; and abstruse operations

Made under certain aspects of the stars,
Producing philtres, to secure the love
Of friends, or death of foes.   We little know,
Groping like children in the dark:—" But O,
I see a vision of hereafter times
Appalling, wonderful, of things to be
Which now cannot be ; a limitation
Rather potential, than real; as where
Th' effect is possible, but time nor place
Nor ground nor matter yield whereon to build.
But notwithstanding these precincts and bounds
I here foretell, and let appeal thereof
Be made to time, that there remaineth yet
A world of unknown science and invention
So far above the known, that all the realms
Of ancient knowledge with the new compared
Will seem but barbarous." *

 GAS. I feel it must be so.

 DUKE.   To the present:
Nephew, I will possess you with a drug
Of potent virtue, by whose operation
And occult qualities, your dear mother
Shall be restored to your father's love,
And you to Isabel's ; a remedy

* A literal prophecy of Bacon's.

For your double grief. Await me here.

      (*Exit to laboratory, music heard.*)

  GAS. I've heard of such things, but believ'd them not;
It cannot work; love is an effluence
Of Deity and cannot be compell'd.
Say it succeed; either it must be by
Commotion in the blood, and therefore earthly;—
Or by the magic aid of spirits evil;
Compulsion most unholy. Isabel,
Not such the love I crave,—and yet—oh yet—

     Re-enter DUKE.

  DUKE.   'Tis done.
Gaston, these philtres are of different strength;
To th' age and nature of the patient meted;
This pouncet box a present give from me
To Isabel, and soon the hop'd effect,
The fruitful harvest of her love you'll reap.
This gilded phial with more caution use:
To your father, whether in wine or food
Administer'd, it will restore his love
To your dear mother; keep it most secret;
Confide in no man. Altho' it is to save
Your mother's life, yet act as though it held
Your father's death; for he is suspicious
And in his anger quick, and might not brook
Being tamper'd with.

GAS.   I will be secret.

Farewell, dear uncle.

DUKE.   Gaston, my son, farewell! [*Exit* GASTON.

He's doom'd; and yet he is a peerless man.

Had he not wrong'd me!—The Earl being dead,

Gaston must needs his coronet assume,

By right his heir: but say, by some mischance

His secret come abroad, 'twould be for rats,

Or for some distant foe, or for—himself:

No mind could aim the true intent; so much

They love each other. Ha! my hand has arm'd

Th' innocent son's hand 'gainst his father's life:

No matter, a double vengeance. Mock on,

While I Jove's lightning power wield, and strike

Unseen; and then my triumph comes!

—— o ——

SCENE 6.—*Ortaise. The Platform of the Castle. Moonlight.*

GASTON.

He told me it was harmlesss, yet I like it not

To practice on my father with these charms;

I have no faith in them; or if I had,

Or did he know that I had dared so far

To tamper with him! that was the Duke's word.

I would do much dear mother, to restore

Thee to his love; this is too perilous

To honour as to life.   To Isabel—
That box sent openly will show, if aught
Of virtue it possess, but the other—
No—this I will not use—but closely keep.
True, my brother saw it, and my manner
May in him have raised some suspicion ;
Reckless he is, but honest—yet caution !
O Isabel, would I were dead,—now,—now
That all hope is gone.   Yet were 't possible
This charm could move the fixed soul,—O no !
No !—misery, misery, misery !
O I am weary, I'll go try and rest.

> *(Retires by the door of the turret.)*
> *Enter* EVAIN.

    EVA. This is some mystery, else why from me
Conceal it ; yes, and with such violence ?
It is not like him, he's ever gentle.
Unravel it I will—now that he sleeps.
Will he, nill he, I will be satisfied.

> *(Enters the turret room and returns.)*

Here it is—a gilt lachrymatory.
H'm ! a powder in it,—what may this be ?
I'll make bold to take a sample :
I have it—if it should be so—I'm made :
Hist, he stirs within, I must restore the—

> *(Enters as before.)*

And now

To the proof, I have some puppies in the mews ;

On them I'll try it. *[Exit.*

(*Enter two Warders, meeting.*)

1st War. Good night ! heard you the spirits' wail ?

2nd War. What spirit ? the spirit of red wine is
humming in your ears : I heard nought.

1st War. Listen—listen !

(*Wild distant music heard.*)

Re-enter Evain.

Eva. To your rounds, men. (*They retire.*)

'Tis as I thought—Poison !

Now from this to weave my fortunes : poor fool !

He loves Isabel, but she loves not him :

But why she should in preference love me,

Save from perversity of womankind,

I know not : but now to my plot. All's won.

——o——

Scene 7.—*The Castle Hall.*

The Earl of Foix.

Earl. The Bishop of Lascalles it seems at Pau

Is hatching mischief : well, let him beware ;

The Pope himself shall not deliver him

If he prove false. This were a business

For Gaston : the monk will despise his youth,
And thus be off his guard.

Enter EVAIN.

EVA.　　　　　　　　　　Good morrow, sir.

EARL. Where's your brother?

EVA.　　　　　　　　He's just now ridden forth
In angry mood ; he is much chang'd ;—'tis since
He came back from Navarre ; he's sullen grown ;
Scarce speaks, and seems no longer like a brother.

EARL. What is the cause bethink you ?

EVA.　　　　　　　　　May be, love :
Isabel looks coldly on his suit 'tis said.

EARL. Tut, she knows our will ; he has nought to
　　fear.

EVA. Then I know not, unless some discontent
From the Duke's court brought back his heart has
　　chang'd
Towards us.

EARL.　　　How ! how ! now you slander him.

EVA. My lord, you asked me what I thought ; my
　　guess
I've frankly told you ; that is,—I mean,—yet
After all 'tis but my blind surmise.

EARL. And yet—Evain, I've watched your looks ;
　　if he
Is mutable you've caught his fickle mood ;

Your face is like a cornfield under wind,
Wave chasing wave, shifting from thought to thought;
'Tis not your wont : you have some painful birth
That struggles to break forth, and still you pause
And hesitate to give it utterance.

EVA. My lord, 'tis true : my heart is torn between
The duty to my father that I owe,
And my poor brother's love.

EARL.   I charge you, speak !
Stay, Gaston shall be present and hear all.

EVA. Pardon me my lord, if Gaston come
I speak not.

EARL.   Ha ! and why ?

EVA.   I may be wrong,
And would not he should know of my suspicion :
And O, dear father, promise that no step
Until th' occasion offer you will take,
Else might it be said I had accused him
For my own ends : proof easy can be made,
And happy shall I be if he prove true.

EARL. Well, Evain, your honour I promise you
Shall suffer no attaint : if plot there be,
I in my own time will unravel it.

EVA. Under that pledge I speak : My lord, you know
Gaston and I are lodged in the rooms
Within the turret in the eastern wing ;

Two days ago when we retired to rest,
From his cast doublet a small packet fell,
A velvet pouch, embroidered round with gold:
I banter'd him 'twas some true love token
From a new fair friend, and tried to see it:
Never man saw I so mov'd; over his face
The red blood mounted dark; then livid wrath,
Like a white squall seething the deep Garonne,
Left it all pale: I thought he would have stabbed me:
Soon he recovered; put away the cause,
And laugh'd it off, but with so bad a grace,
Suspicion seized me and held me restless
Throughout the weary night, revolving how
To solve this mystery. I know not if
'Twere right; I thought it was: last night he slept
Sound as a babe—scarcely so innocent:
In fine I found the pouch, open'd it, but
No love token found: a gilded phial
With a white powder fill'd I saw; he mov'd;
Quick I replac'd it and in haste withdrew.

    EARL. And you believe that this was—was—

    EVA.   Poison!
Else why this dread of showing it to me
His brother? why these moods, and short-cut speech?
He show'd you all his presents from Navarre,
Did he show you this?

EARL.   Poison ! but for whom ?

He has no enemies ; or if he had

He'd dare them openly ; he may have been

Palter'd with ; 'tis like.

EVA.   And most probable.

He has some heavy weight upon his mind,

And once or twice unwittingly has said

His lady mother should again be in

Your favour, or more honour'd than before.

EARL. Peace ! no more, show this to no living man !

EVA. I'm dumb : 'tis now in your own hands : th'
    evening

Banquet may give the opportunity.

Grant heav'n it prove some folly, or my fear.

EARL. 'Tis against my nature ; but I've promised,

And will wait : leave me. (*Exit* EVAIN.) I dare not
    believe it.

Gaston ? my son ? God ! 'tis impossible !   [*Exit.*

ACT III.

SCENE 1.—*Ortaise.   The Banquet Hall.*

CHAMBERLAIN, HALBERT, *Servants, &c.*

CHAM. Quick, knaves, be more alert, set on: if the Earl has to wait, some of you will sit i' the stocks for it, or worse.

1ST SER. And if he hasn't what shall we get? small reward, I trow.

CHAM. Saucy loon! when you've earn'd thanks, crave them; that will be some 29th of February; that day was invented for such rare occasions.   Come, Halbert, help lad.   Roast quarry is better than 'live to hawk at.

HAL. That will I, master Chamberlain, the rather that I see a good feed of broken vietuals beyond, to tire on.   Hear you how fares Sir Ernalton?

CHAM. Badly, they say; a good knight, Sir Ernalton, a good knight, he cannot live; when the Earl strikes he strikes home: work knaves, work; here they come and nought fair!•

Enter THE EARL, GASTON, EVAIN, SIR MAULÉON, SIR
AIMERY, SIR JOHN FROISSART, *Lords, Knights,*
Squires, and Attendants.

EARL. Welcome friends; sit knights and gentlemen.
Sir John, my want of courtesy of late
I pray you pardon; still these state affairs
Will ever cross our path at undue times.
How fares the Earl of Namur, your good lord?

FROI. No excuse there needs. Sir Robert is in
health.   (*They sit.*)

EARL. Sir, I thank you: to all good appetite.
Chamberlain, to the other boards take heed,
See them well serv'd. Free may we be this day
From enemies, and domestic traitors;
From these no man is safe. Gaston, the cup!
Some wine!

(GASTON *as cupbearer stooping to present the tankard,*
puts his hand to the breast of his doublet.)
What hide you, son?

GAS.   Nothing, my lord,
Worth note.

EARL.   Some love token? you pale fair son!
What is 't?

GAS. Oh no—yes—will you take the cup?

EARL. Why shakes your hand thus? Why this
confusion?

There's more in this. Give me—that! what? I
    wait!

Gas. Take it, my lord, and marvel not that I
Should hesitate light follies to confess
In presence of this public company.

Earl. Say you so? what's here? a gilded phial:
H'm! now I remember me—yes, 'tis so.

Gas. Dear father, what troubles you? why muse you
So frowningly?

Earl. Peace! what ho! Sir Chamberlain!
Bring here a mess of meat. Put down the cup:
'Twill be full time—afterwards.

Cham.   My lord is served.

(*The* Earl *opens the phial and scatters the powder over
    the meat.*)

Earl. Here, Sanglier! you're old like your master,
Poor hound, and can be spar'd, should the meat prove
Your last meal.

(*The hound devours the mess, falls down writhing in
    convulsions, and dies. The company rise in con-
    fusion, the* Earl *stands frowning on his son, his
    hand on his dagger,* Gaston *gazing on the scene
    with intense horror.*)

Gas. Merciful heav'n! this is too horrible!

    (*With sudden calm he turns to the crowd.*)

If there is here a knight or gentleman

Will do my errand for the love of God,

O fly! the Lady Isabel! O haste!

She has the counterpart! Save—O save her—

  EVA.   Damnation! (*Rushes out.*)

  GAS. And I may be her murderer. Hold brain!

           (*He falls on his knee.*)

I thank thee, God, that thou hast sav'd

My soul from this dark stain : my every nerve

Quivers ; and my blood congeals to think

Of the abyss of crime from which I've 'scaped.

Parricide! I! a father so beloved!

Great God! I dream : it is impossible!

Father, dear, dear father! hear me! I swear

By all the sacred host, my hopes of heaven,

That of this foul attempt I'm innocent

As when a babe I nestled in your arms.   (*Rising.*)

God! he believes me not!

  EARL. See you, my lords, and hear you this viper?

Whose conscience stronger even than his cunning

Has forced confession from him. You have heard

This poison was for me alone, and yet

With ready tongue he dares to call upon

His God to witness to his innocence.

Taken with the red hand! 'tis past all sense

And seeming! A man to carry poison

In his bosom, and not know it deadly!

And yet I dream'd he lov'd me; nor would I
Upon the witness of a host of tongues,
Have judg'd him capable of doing aught
To give me one moment's pain.　Sure I am
Was never father lov'd a son more truly;
And this foul fault in him all filial love
Must stamp hypocrisy; must all fathers
Render fearful.　O boy! was it for this,
Ungrateful! that I've toil'd to leave a state
That monarchs envy for thine heritage?
Was it for this that I have spar'd thy blood,
And shed mine own, keeping thee from wars
And perils threatful to thine unform'd youth,
More as a mother cherishes her child;
That thou in guilty ease might'st hatch thy plots
Against a life whose every pulse was thine?

GAS. Spare me, O my father! spare me
These upbraidings, which keener pierce
My prostrate spirit than could your dagger.
But, O my father! think, for you are wise:
If I were guilty, should I unprepar'd,
Confess th' intent, when plausibly I might,
A tale devise that the vile drug was meant
For vermin, or an enemy, or for—

FROI. True! innocence alone could thus blaze forth
The truth, when truth is death.

Gas. If you knew all?

Earl. Enough I know; the plot has fail'd. Wert
 thou
A common man, the torture should ere this
Have rack'd thy limbs, before the gibbet felt
Thy weight. My son,—no meaner hand than mine
Shall slay thee.
Art thou prepared, nor does thy coward blood
Forsake thy cheek to look on death?

Gas. O no; a son of Foix can never blench
With fear: but horror, horror! strike father!
Justice demands it: strike!

Earl. Justice? but now you said that you were
 innocent,
Die. (*offers to strike*) God! when I look upon his face
I cannot do it.

Gas. Strike: yet one word more:
Dear father did you ever know me lie?
Innocent I am! So God do to me
And more, if I a thought e'er harboured
Of you that was not love. Yet I'd not live:
No, slay me, O my father, for I feel
Incrusted with a leprosy of guilt;
To be the tool, the weak unwitting tool
To deal so dread a parricidal blow.
God forgive them that arm'd my hand and left

No shield for my lost soul. Father, O strike!

Better to die, and by so dear a hand,

Than live dishonour'd by so dark a stain.

 EARL. 'Tis true :—die then— (*about to strike.*)

 FROI. Stay ; pardon, my lord: there is more in
  this,

Not only as regards your proper person,

But as affects the safety of your state :

It were well to know, for I do believe

That he is innocent, who laid this plot,

Of which at least he is the instrument.

Meanwhile ; my lord be kept in custody.

 GAS. Sir John, I thank thee not: better that I

Had died a happy death, than be compell'd

T' unravel this dark—O my dear mother!

 EARL. Thy mother!

 GAS.   Oh no, alas!

 EARL.   What mean you?

Danger to me from thence?

 GAS. No father, I but thought of her great grief,

When she shall hear her only child is dead.

     Enter EVAIN.

O what of Isabel? lives she yet?

 EVA.   Safe ;

Or thou wert not now alive to ask it:

The drug was harmless!

EARL.   Harmless, this is strange.

GAS. I thank thee brother, nathless your churlish
   speech

To one whom God has smitten, and your brother:

Do you love her? O then, I forgive you.

EARL. See him in safe custody: in private

We will enquire further.   [*Exeunt.*

GAS. And she loves him: O now my vision clears,

Here standing on the confines of the tomb,

To the full scope of all my misery.

Yes, from a brother's hand this bolt has fall'n:

For love of Isabel was I betray'd:

It did not need; for mine is not a heart

To be contented with an outward form

Without the soul; for me she loved not,

Else had not come upon me this great woe;

But no, another aim has prompted you

To what you then but guess'd, tho' now prov'd sooth

Would reach my life,—a blood-stain'd coronet!

Yet I thank thee.   But for this wrong intent

How deep a gratitude were due to you.

I thank thee brother, from my inmost heart,

That thou hast sav'd my soul from parricide,

Aiming to pour this ruin on my head.

O Isabel, 'twill grieve your gentle breast

To know you are the prize of villainy,

                                        X

As deep as hell—you and my heritage.

And I !—O fool !—yet how could I e'en dream

So dread a horror?   What? my uncle arm

Mine, his nephew's hand, 'gainst my own father?

What devil taught you bait your treachery

With mother's love?   O it was learnt in hell:

No human brain could plan such sacrilege.

My brain reels to think on 't, or take it in !

O that I were dead! which soon I shall be.

Enter RAYMONET.

RAY. My lord, I come to show you to your lodging :
Will 't please you go?

GAS.   Ay, my narrow lodging,
'Twill be my last; lead on.   [*Exeunt.*

——o——

SCENE 2.—*Hotel d'Armagnac, Ortaise.   A Drawing
room.*

ISABEL, PAULINE.

PAU. O my lady, have you heard the news?   I am
so frighted.   There was an uproar at the banquet last
night; I fear to tell you.

ISA. O speak out: from whom heard you this?

PAU. From Halbert, he was there in waiting, helping
the serving-men.

Isa. And making love to the waiting maids: never blush, Pauline: he's a tall youth.

Pau. Madam, an under falconer!

Isa. He may tower, like his hawks: but to your tale.

Pau. Well, there was a plot discover'd, and the Earl stabb'd his son.

Isa. God of Heav'n! what say you?

Pau. Lady, forgive me: you pale; 'twas not Sir Evain, but I forget: Sir Gaston he would have slain, but the nobles interposed and sav'd him. He is now imprisoned in the donjon keep; he swears he's innocent; but every one has his own tale, and the truth no one knows, nor what he's charg'd with. 'Tis said the plot was to poison his father at the banquet.

Isa. Peace, woman, what blasphemy is this?
Gaston, the gentle, kind, and loving!
This is horrible! Go, call my page. [*Exit* Pauline.
I am enrag'd that women are so helpless,
I feel as if involv'd in some strange toil,
And cannot forth to seek or find the truth.
First Evain rushes in, terror in 's looks,
And questions me with scant meed of respect
About a pouncet box, with poison in 't;
And hearing that no poison it contain'd,
With sudden joy—as madly rushes out.
Then comes this waiting woman with her tale

Of uproar at the banquet ; and the name
Of Gaston bandied to and fro : still he
The centre of the turmoil ;—whether slain,
Or slayer, I know not, and dread to hear
The truth ;—and yet I must ; all too painful
Is this suspense. (*Enter page.*) Go, run in haste ;
Seek out Sir Mauléon, you will find him
At the Castle, or at his lodging, or
The hostel in Ortaise ; haste, why wait you ?

    PAGE. I wait your message to Sir Mauléon ?

    ISA. O my poor wits, I had forgot ; tell him
The Lady Isabella d'Armagnac,
All business set aside saving the Earl's,
Desires his attendance here forthwith.
Say I await him here ; away !

———o———

SCENE 3.—*The Same.*

ISABEL, SIR MAULÉON.

    ISA. Thanks, thanks Sir Mauléon, for your courtesy,
To come so readily at my request.

    MAU. How ; fail in the chief duty of a knight,
A lady's service !

I should deserve to lose my knightly spurs :
Command me aught within the power of man.

   ISA. In few words.   If no argument of state
Bind you to secresy, I must entreat
That you resolve me all these rumours strange,
That fly distractingly around, into
Some form of truth.

   MAU. Lady, I can do so, but 'tis a task
Of pain.   Can you bear it ?   Can you bear
To hear of those you love in peril
Of death or of dishonour ? it is hard.

   ISA. Sooner or later I must know it all,
Later, with less power to bear than now :
Therefore now.—I will try and force my soul
Up to the pitch.

   MAU. Would it were some other.
Can you bear it now ?

   ISA.   Enough : I will !

   MAU. First I would premise—truly I believe 't—
Sir Gaston of all crime is innocent.

   ISA. Thank heav'n ! dear, dear Gaston,—proceed,
   go on.

   MAU. But an I'm not mistaken, his brother
Sir Evain is a villain !

   ISA.   Ha ! what say you ?
I am better now, go on ; from the first.

MAU. Dear lady, it grieves me thus to pain you,
Still I obey.   Gaston late returned
From the Countess, his mother, in Navarre;
Since when he's noted to be alter'd much.
Last eve, at dinner in the banquet hall
Sir Gaston was his father's cup-bearer,
And stooping to his office—he reveal'd
A packet hidden in his doublet's folds :
Th' Earl demands it; being thereof advis'd :
After some delay 'tis given, and proves
Poison! Awaiting some explanation
Simple of the fact, all in mute amaze
Behold Sir Gaston fall upon his knee,
Horror on his brow, and with ashy lips
Thank God that saved him from parricide.
On this confession the enraged Earl
His dagger drew, and would have slain his son:
But the father—could not—albeit his son
Pleaded most hard for death.   He is arrest.
He says he knew not it was poison, is
The tool of others, but withholds their names.
Lady, you are pale, let me now retire.

ISA. No, my sense is numb'd, I can bear more.

MAU. This is all; oh yes, I had forgotten;
There was a box he said he gave to you.
He fear'd was deadly too.   He sent for it.

Isa. He did, go on—

Mau.   This is all.

Isa.   No, not all ;

This is not all, I do remember me

You said Sir Evain was—was— a villain !

As you are true knight hide nothing from me.

   Mau. (*aside*) How's this ? she seems more moved by

      this stain,

Than by the peril her betroth'd is in.

Lady, I come now from the council board ;

The matter discuss'd, it was proved plain

Sir Evain knew his brother had this drug,

And manag'd to prepare his father's mind

For the discovery. He might have warn'd ;

He might have saved him; for well he knew

The deadly nature of—

   Isa.   How knew ? what proof ?

   Mau. One night Sir Evain stole down to the mews,

The falconer saw him feed the bloodhound pup,

Next day he found it dead. Sir Evain thought

The falconer dar'd not speak ; because he knew

That Josselin had disobey'd the Earl's commands.

In vain,—altho' he trembled—he spoke truth.

   Isa. Too much ! too much !—marvel not, Sir Knight,

I am so mov'd : a double grief is heavy,

Either being too much for one weak woman.

A brother, and a suitor at one blow

Lost: to-day—I may bear it.   I am stunned.

But to-morrow, and again to-morrow,

And onward through coming years—how bear it?

Your help to that couch,—so—my thanks, and pray

Strike for my maidens on that bell, farewell.

       [*Exit* Sir Mauléon.

Alas! poor women, that we should be slaves

Of sense or fancy, unreasoning ever:

How we shrink, when men with adulation

Exalt us to their worship's height? Just so

The clay idol, had it sense, would crumble

And fall to ruin: in our inmost heart

We feel the humbling thought: there lurks the fiend,

There coil'd up—with half-clos'd eyes he lies,

Watching the music of the soul to jar

The strings and make all discord; break, we may,

The lute,—never the melody restore.

That is my task.   How could I love this man?

How can I? for I do.   Mysterious fiend

Taking the likeness of the angel love,

How hast thou deceiv'd me with a semblance!

I shame t' appear before the noble heart

Whose love I trifled with; yet fain would fawn

Upon the base hand that has robb'd his life.

But no, he comes—break heart, I will be free!

Enter EVAIN.

EVA. Dear Isabel, my haste when last we met
Made me abrupt, perhaps unmannerly ;
Now, these perils past, you and my father
Sav'd, th' unnatural author of this plot
From further practice safe ; I fly once more
To sun me in the glory of your eyes,
And—how's this ?—you turn away,—Isabel !

  ISA. Hear me, Evain, hear me.

  EVA.   Music—speak !

  ISA.   It will not be long :
Once I knew a maiden of a noble house,
And she lov'd,—I am not good at portraits ;—
She thought not of his parentage or rank,
But to her eyes he seem'd the noblest man
That ever grac'd clos'd lists or tented field.
Time came—her eyes were opened,—she found
Her idol ignoble, false and coward :
What think you she should have done ?

  EVA.   There is none,—
No man, so all bad, that could thus put on
The outward semblance of nobility.
What did she ?

  ISA.   She cast him off !

  EVA. Then she little lov'd.

Isa.   Misery ! how much !

Eva. So earnest : This comes nearer home.

Isa. It does.   Yes, Evain, 'tis to you I speak,
And for each word that my pain'd lips let fall
Fall drops of blood from my oppressed heart.
When I look upon you you are the same,
To my soul's clear sight you are another :
Mine eyes still lead me captive to a thrall
My soul abhors.   I thought you noble,
Now I see you base ! I thought you true,
And now I know you false ! Brave I deem'd you :
How have you prov'd a coward : Fratricide !

Eva. Why do you charge me thus ? why thus
    accuse
Of crimes undreamt ?   What man hath slander'd me ?
On his head I'll prove I am no coward.
And you to believe all—shows not much love.

Isa. Yet all's true :—you do not dare deny it :
And yet I'm glad, if for aught that's evil
I can rejoice, that you show no contrition ;
Had you but shown some sorrow for the deed ;
Did you repent the ruin you have caused ;
My heart might yet have fix'd upon one spot,
One bright spot in a dark and desert void,
Where love might cling as to a slippery rock
In ocean, though the next moment swept it

Into th' abyss.   Honest you are—in ill :
And I thank you : you leave me nought to love :
Thus I cast you off! I would be alone!

   Eva. Isabel, hear me ! dear, dear Isabel !

   Isa. I would be alone!   [*Exit* Evain.

             I breathe—'tis done,
And he is gone : yes, I feel a stern joy
In my triumph.   Given up so easily ?
My weaker nature rises at this slight :
He lov'd me not, or he had sued and prayed
And pour'd out all his soul in agony ;
And I—for I am woman—had believed
And scarce had conquer'd.   No, he lov'd me not,
And now I feel his once so prized image
Limn'd in false colours fading from my heart ;
O baffl'd craven ! taken by surprise,
He had nor time, nor thought to counterfeit.
O Gaston !
How does your chief of loyalty o'ertop
His base! How does your true and noble love
Rush music-like into my vacant soul,
Left desert of his false.   Now to save him.

ACT IV.

SCENE 1.—*The Donjon.*

GASTON.

GAS. Come death, come gentle death, thou art much
    wrong'd ;
Come succour me with thy soft painless hand,
Relieve me from the wreck of my lost life.
And what is death ? from the first breathing time
Until we cease to be is all one death :
And yet the mind clogg'd by the flesh still shrinks,
While trembling on the verge of the unknown,—
The undefin'd,—and fears some dread convulsion.
Before the proof how all such fears must fade.
See. we men die, by violence, sickness ;
The pain is from the wound or the disease ;
How many sink to death with infant calm,
Or senseless struck down by a sudden blow ;
So a man stricken by a serpent's fang
Scarce feels the wound, but soon his blood congeals,
His heart grows still and cold, his wondrous frame

Falls venom-struck unpain'd a lifeless heap ;
Like a bright flower cut from its parent stem,
Soon as its sap fails ebbing fast away
Droops all its leaves and bloom, of life forlorne.
How many drown'd and rescued who ne'er felt
A pang :—perchance their spirits parted not
From their lov'd tenement ? Then reason thus :
'Tis clear unto the mind the death we fear
Is but a line invisible 'tween this
Our present state and that which shall be ;
A non-existent point, incapable
Of suffering : It follows then this pang
Is suffered by the body—or—the soul :
If by the body it is but the pain
Of the disease,—greater we feel—yet live,
And this must cease when the two separate.
If the soul suffer pain—we know not ;
But this we know, it is no longer death.
No, like an eagle from a skyey crag
Launch'd on broad vanes into the vast of space,
What may constrict that essence rarefied
We know not ; but sure it is not death.
Were life the precious gem the vulgar hold,
'Twould not so lightly be cast off—or perill'd
Not only for great ends, for faith, for king,
Or country ; but for sport, emulation,

For a light word or for a wanton's smile,
Men brave this cold-blood terror.   What remains ?
Death is the occupation of a life,
And when life ceases then we cease to die
And truly live.   Like the bright gorgeous fly
That bursts the sphered cerement of the worm,
And rises on the sunny blue expanse,
We spring unbaffl'd by this fleshly shell,
Glorious creatures—escaped—renovate,
To our long lost element restored.
And O the joy—the ecstasy to feel
Our dim eyes clearing in the sun of truth,
Th' expanding powers,—joys unutterable
Of the perfect being dwelling in love
And peace.   O come ! I will not call thee death ;
But cease O weary body, cease to breathe
To feel !

Enter HALBERT *with food.*

Set it down there—the other take away.
[This pain is milder—easier by habit.]

HAL. My lord, you have not touch'd it.

GAS. Is this a place to gain an appetite ?
It pleases me to fast.   Prithee Halbert,
You were a falconer ; why left you the mews
To turn man-at-arms with steel cap and sword ?

HAL. A tame life my lord, for a man of my inches,

to do nothing but train kites ; true, idleness favour'd
contemplation, but I was ambitious.

GAS. Of what? of broken bones, or cross-bow bolt?
And your contemplations—whither led they?

HAL. Further than my poor speech will help me tell
   you.

GAS. Yet try ! 'twill pass the time.
I stand in need of some philosophy :
Yours for want of better ; 'twill not be platonic.

HAL. Good, and from me ; well, an you wish to
hear : Halbert said I, how long stop you here on
small wage and broken victual? Well 'tis safe. A
mean argument : so said I, soar, soar high enough—
you'll strike some quarry,—a hern mayhap.

GAS. And you being but a kestril
Mayhap get spik'd on the hern's bill.

HAL. I thought of that ; no play without stakes' ;
and then I ponder'd thus : What is life? The past a
sleep : the present a dream. The glimpses of the
past are as when one wakes and tries to catch a lost
dream ; we hold nothing ; dream for dream I try for
the best and may win.

GAS. You care not how ; for the means.

HAL. Means? does any man care for means? I see
men tread on each other's necks, none place their hand
to be walked over : in a crowd who thinks of the mass?
—the end is all.

GAS. I would not trust you for a follower:
You seem incapable of gratitude.

HAL. Gratitude! I have heard of that; have you
ever met with it? 'twould make the fortune of a show
at a fair for rarity. True, we love (at the time) those
who benefit us; is that gratitude? not a bit—stark
selfishness; for—give a man drop by drop ninety-nine
parts of your heart's blood—O, he is so grateful:
refuse him the hundredth—all turns to water: but for
good, honest, unblushing ingratitude commend me to a
woman; and then the giver, he either confers benefits
for his own ends, selfishness again; or he gives for the
pleasure of giving, self-love. Let him enjoy it—but
what right has he to expect thanks? Gratitude!
Bah!

GAS. If your spear bites as sharp as does your
        tongue
Man-at-arms is your calling; you have seen
Far into one side of human nature,
Not the best. Tell me what think you of love?

HAL. Love! ha, ha, excuse my mirth; love is a
mere disease like the measles; it is worse than some,
for it can be caught more than once. There should be
doctors for those attack'd, and hospitals, instead of
which the infected go about like lepers, showing their
sores to excite pity. [Loss of appetite is a symptom—
aside.] For how long think you my lord, you can

live on air ?   These five days I have taken away what
I brought, save what the mice ate.

GAS. Halbert, I like not your philosophy ;
I'd not prolong this dream : I would not live
In your world.

HAL.   That is not brave.

GAS. Then courage 'scapes your tooth;   a dog's
      virtue.

Now in your enlighten'd cogitations
What is honesty ?

HAL. Bah ! not much ; I would not be a full purse
in's way.   Farewell my lord, I'm called.   [*Exit.*

GAS. Alas, he is a true interpreter :
Such is the world ; at love, virtue, honour,
Men stare ; generosity, except
Towards themselves, is mere wanton folly ;
Magnanimity to them is madness,
And gain is all in all.

———o———

SCENE 2.—*The Castle Court.*

Enter HALBERT *and* MAULÉON.

MAU. Halbert well met : how fares your prisoner ?

HAL. He's lunatic—is bent to imitate
The ancient Roman, him who held his life

Y

A property to be put off at will :

Food he refuses ; smiles at pain and death,

And moralises on its incidents.

Mau. How long is this ?

Hal.   Since he was first arrest.

Mau. Six days ! why told you not of this before ?

Hal. I thought he dared not do it ; then I thought

'Twould save the Earl the trouble of his death.

Mau. You thought—and thought ; O will you never
      learn

'Tis not a soldier's part to think but act ?

Hal. But being gifted with a restless brain

Unsuitable it seems to my condition,

It needs must work.   Captain, I've often thought

'Twere better I were raised to some post

Where heads are of more value.

Mau.   Rais'd say you ?

Beware you are not razed by a head ;

'Tis like to guide you to no better end.

To your office : I will see the prisoner.   [*Exeunt.*

—— o ·——

Scene 3.—*The Donjon.*

Enter Mauléon *and* Halbert, *who retires.*

Gas. (*aside*) Oh ! these pangs ! much longer they
      cannot last.

Mau. My lord, you've known me ever for your friend.

Gas. Yes, and a true one.   Welcome, Sir Mauléon.

Mau. My welcome is late timed unless my help
Your lost strength could restore:—how weak you seem,
My dear lord.

Gas.   I am weak ; (*aside.* Still these pangs ;
When will these sufferings cease ? this racking pain
And deadly faintness almost conquer me :)
But death will soon end all, it nears the heart.

Mau. O my dear lord, throw not away your life :
'Tis sinful, and a want of courage shows
To battle with the troubles of the world.

Gas. Sinful, O no, why say you it is sinful ?
There is no law against it : do not die
Is nowhere said.   Courage I have to bear
Fierce pain and injury and blighted love,
Friend's falsehood, loss of wealth, infirmity ;
The spirit of a man supports it all ;
All :—but a wounded spirit who can bear ?
My father pass'd a righteous sentence on me,
And I am but his executioner.

Mau. O no ; be sure he wishes not your death.

Gas. But I will not retain my forfeit life.
My dear friend 'tis enough.   I'm near the bourne,
This anguish soon will cease.

Mau.   The Earl must know this.

GAS. Why should he know it? Wait till I am dead,
And should it grieve him—for he loved me,
Speak gently to him, tell him 'tis better
For me—best for him—that thus it should be.
Tell him of one who could—O this faintness—
Who could have lived or died for his glory,
But—oh !—who will not live to bring him shame.

[Exeunt.

——o——

SCENE 4.—*A Room in the Castle.*

Enter the EARL *and* SIR JOHN FROISSART.`

EARL. I know not—ho ! there ! *(Enter Attendant)*
　　has Sir Mauléon come?

ATT. He has my lord, and waits.

EARL. 　　　　　　　　Admit him here.
I know not what to think, 'tis past belief
The boy could hatch a plot—a deadly plot
Against my life; alone : 'tis past belief:

Enter SIR MAULÉON.

Sir Mauléon, those prisoners on suspicion,
Have they been confronted with Sir Gaston ?

MAU. They have my lord, but no clue could I gain
To solve the mystery ; he declares them
Innocent, absolves them of all knowledge :
But heard you yet, my lord, your son's resolve ?

EARL. Has he resolved t' unload his charged heart
Of this unnatural conspiracy ?

MAU. Oh no !

EARL.   What then ?

MAU.   The tale I dread to tell.

EARL. Trifle not with me, speak ! I must know all.

MAU. He has resolved to die.

FROI.   How, by 's own hand ?

EARL. Yes ? this must not be : but to prevent it ;
See that no means be left within his reach,
No arms, no—let every man be search'd
That to him has access or brings him food :
Under this durance if he fret 'twere well
To give him hopes of our clemency.

MAU. Alas my lord, the prison irks him not ;
It is the prison of the flesh whose bars
Encage him with dishonour ; he brooks not
This horror nor will bear it.

EARL.   'Tis most like :
Die ! he shall not :—Sir Mauléon, see to it ;
Your life for his, if aught befall him ill.

FROI. Pardon my lord, he is not in his hands, .
Nor can you claim his life—of man. You have
The power of death, not life : you may kill
But God alone can save alive ; nor you—
Nor I.—Think you so frail a thing

As life may not be parted with at will?
A thing accessible to every chance:
The north wind slays it with an icy sword;
The south wind rots it with a deadly breath;
A stylet's point can plume the ruddy wings
On which flies forth the eager 'scaping life:
A little water or a little fire
Soon finds it lurking in its unknown cave
And stops its breathings.   You may remove
All outward means, yet the determined will
Rules royally within the realm of life,
And finds its own time to send forth its subject.

 Mau. My lord, the evil is past remedy.

 Earl. He is not dead?

 Mau.   No, but dying; six days
No food has pass'd those closed lips on which
Is fixed the stern smile of a calm resolve:
But while his body faints his heav'n lit eyes
Are bright with glories of eternity.

 Earl. Why was I not told of this? I have been
Too stern; he must be sav'd.

 Froi.   Sir, there are few
Would venture on you with an ill report,
And all believe you wish your son were dead,
Waiting to greet you as with welcome news.

 Earl. You are bitter Sir John, and some might say

Your words were contradicted by the fact,
When you can move me thus and see me calm.

FROI. I am but a poor scholar, yet I've found
In many travels both by land and sea,
In princes' court or in the robbers' hold,
[Small difference between the two, I ween]
'Mong men of every grade I've ever found
That the best passport through the world is truth.
I am your well wisher and guest,—and you
Have with some show of friendship honour'd me,
For which I am your debtor,—and for this
My duty counsels me to countervail
Aught that affects your int'rest or safety,
Or militates against your fair earn'd fame ;
If I offend I pray you pardon me.

EARL. Your frankness I excuse ; and yet I doubt
The power of your talisman. What then
Becomes of policy, of caution, judgment,
Or expediency ? Truth ! the current coin
Of those who have no other : with nought to lose
Men can afford the truth, but those in power
Would short lease enjoy of their possessions
If lips were not the hypocrites of hearts.
I will see this boy. Let him be told so.

MAU. My lord, I will prepare him.

[*Exeunt.*

SCENE 5.—*The Donjon.*

GASTON *alone.*

My mind no longer wanders ;

No more pain : I had thought to have suffered more.

How many a wretch upon the landless sea,

Or lost in the primeval forest's maze,

Has gone through greater pain barb'd by the fear

Of death ; while I am lighten'd by its hope.

But now 'tis past and weakness weighs me down ;

Fail not my will ; soar 'bove the body's strength,

And bear me to the goal ; be hardest steel

To the sharp arrows of a father's grief ;

Melt not at Isabel's eye-fountain'd tears,

Tears that might lure a hero to his death,

But me not back to life.   Dear Isabel !

Is it not strange how much we love each other ?

O why is true love trammell'd by this clay ?

Hereafter 'twill not be so ; then no need

To analyse the species of each love ;

The love of sister, mother, child or wife,

What are they but one heavenly harmony

Breathing from different earthly instruments ?

When these are broken then all love is one ;

Love ! that pure atmosphere that angels breathe

Around the throne of God.

Enter the EARL.

Dear father, I would rise and kneel to you,
But that my weakened body helps me not
To act the homage that my true heart feels.

EARL. Ungrateful boy; is this a meet return
For my forbearance?   What is this I hear?
Is it for you—if you are innocent
Of this most damned plot—is it for you   '
To die and lay your blood upon my head?
Or guilty—does remorse so sting your soul
You dare not live to bear the infamy?

GAS. O my father, yet a little while forbear,
For little time I've left for suffering;
Upbraid me not, for life is waning fast,
And I would wish to part in love with all.

EARL. But is it now too late?   O you were wrong!

GAS. It is.   No power of man could save me now.

EARL. O this is bitter!

GAS.   Dear father, grieve not:
Better for me,—for all,—but if you still
Feel love for me—O spare the innocent;
Let no man suffer for fault which is mine
Alone.

EARL. How is't to be known?—not knowing
Who are the guilty; see you not that you   '

Place them by concealment in this peril?

This is not just, nor is it right to leave me

In ignorance of whence this danger comes;

Or drifting on the current of suspicion

Friends I may wound when I should strike my foes.

    GAS. Father, this is most true—yet how reveal

So dread a secret? (*aside.* Yet I owe him nought

For me he recklessly betrayed to death.)

E'en my dear mother might not 'scape th' attaint.

    EARL. No, and duty to her, to me, to all

Must still persuade confession of the truth

Which 'gins to dawn upon me.

    GAS.   What think you?

My mother is most innocent.

    EARL.   Her brother?

    GAS. You have said.   He told me 'twas a philtre

To reinstal my mother in your love.

Then spare the rest who nothing know; enough

Is one victim.   This load from off my mind,

I happier feel.   Father! you believe me?

    EARL. O my poor boy, how have you been betrayed;

I never injur'd him and he has plann'd

This deed for covetise to save his gold.

I should have warned you against the schemes

The dev'lish schemes of this most wily Duke.

But to lose you?   Surely 'tis not too late.

GAS. Oh yes, too late, too late !

Enter ISABEL *and* PAULINE.

ISA.   O why is this ?

And I—I have done this ! Beloved Gaston,

O leave us not; O live ! I would have time

To pour my heart's repentance at your feet.

GAS. O, angel vision ! Death is surely past !

O love ! still clings to me this flesh although

Refin'd by the attenuated frame :

Dear Isabel !

ISA.   Beloved, I am free !

Free from the serpent coil that kept me from you.

O how could I have cared for one so vile ?

It was not love ! O how could I thus kill

A noble heart ?—Gaston I do love you.

O my beloved, live ! Is there no hope ?

O Gaston, for the love I bear you, live !

GAS. Patience dear Isabel ! 'tis very sweet

To know even now that you return my love :

So in heav'n we'll meet and claim each other.

For here,—it boots not think what might have been.

ISA. I have kill'd you ! O my beloved, live !

And save me, save me from this dread remorse :

Alas, O woe is me ! what have I done ?

GAS. Not so, my darling ; O believe it not :
Although when lost your love, death was a boon ;
I could have liv'd—and hop'd—and suffer'd on,
Yet I could not survive, dear Isabel,
My honour dead.   It would have clung to me,
This infamy,—and were you mine,—to you
In all your innocence and purity.
Therefore uplift this weight from off your soul
That you are cause of my self-sacrifice.
Altho' your love 'bove every earthly good
I prize, I would not link your lot—with—with
A parricide ! I've said it : how it burns
Into my soul ;—God's mercy rase it out !
Kiss me Isabel, for when God forgives—
I'm failing fast—an angel may surely love.
Support me love ; in death alone, my wife :
I'm very weak,—on your bosom,—my head,—
Heav'n and earth are meeting ! O Isabel !
Wife ! darling ! O so happy !—to die thus :
Weep not, dear father ;—shall we not soon meet
Above ?   Dearest Isabel O go not !
Hold—hold me ; I feel going ;—now I see
A seraph bending o'er me with bright wings !
O, 'tis you ! open your arms—receive me :
Wide ! wide ! to your heart ! Isabel—thus—Oh !

                                    (*Dies.*)

(*Isabel sinks on her knees beside him : gazes on*
his face long and fixedly ; then embraces
him and lays her head on his breast.)

EARL. Come, Isabel, henceforth my child—arise
And come with me.   My punishment is more
Than I can bear.   Come with me Isabel :
Bring her away—gently, poor child—gently.

PAU. My lord, she'll come no more ; her spirit's fled
With his.   She is dead! her heart has broken.

EARL. Dead! said you dead ?—O grief!—it cannot
    be !
My son!—my child !—both dead ! and I am left
Alone !

(*He covers his face and weeps.*)

Scene closes.

NOTES.

Page 12, line 9.

Had I but said, I would have kept my word !
But when I swear, it is irrevocable.

SHAKESPEARE.

Page 93, line 3.

See how my sword weeps for the poor king's death.

SHAKESPEARE.

Page 150, line 18.

There is a resemblance in this to a passage in
" Elaine," but my homely picture was composed long
before I had seen that beautiful poem.

Page 155, line 9.

His silver skin lac'd with his golden blood.

SHAKESPEARE.

Page 177, line 15.

How can frail pen describe her heavenly grace
For fear for lack of skill her beauty to deface.

SPENSER.

Page 183, line 4.

Most ignorant of what he's most assured,
His glassy essence.   SHAKESPEARE.

Page 195, line 16.

At every fall smoothing the raven down
Of darkness till it smil'd.   MILTON.

Page 215, line 14.

Like Niobe all tears.   SHAKESPEARE.

I have ventured to quote Niobe as an example of another
phase in the passion of grief. The ancients fabled her as
turned to stone.

LIST OF SUBSCRIBERS.

———•◊•———

Mrs. Roy Adams, Tunbridge Wells.

Mr. Tyssen Amhurst, Didlington.   6 copies.

Mrs. Tyssen Amhurst,   ,,   6 copies.

Mr. Anderson, Little Harle Tower.

Mr. John Anderson, Newcastle-on-Tyne.

Mr. Atkinson, Angerton.

Mrs. Atkinson,   ,,

Mr. Wilson-Atkinson, Acton House.

Mrs. Wilson-Atkinson,   ,,

Mr. Atkinson, Wylam Hall.

Sir Edward Blackett, Bart., Matfen.

Mrs. W. C. Boodle, 33, Connaught Square.   3 copies.

Mrs. T. Salkeld Bramwell, Jesmond Dene House.
    2 copies.

Mrs. Brooke, Taney Hill House, Dundrum, Co. Dublin.

The Rev. Dixon Brown, Unthank Hall.

Mrs. Dixon Brown,   ,,

Mrs. Brown, Houghton.

Mr. Ralph Brown, Whickham.

Mrs. Ralph Brown,   ,,

Mrs. T. Brown, Mitford.

Miss M. Brown, ,,

Mr. Brumell, Morpeth.

Mrs. Brumell, ,,

Mr. M. Brumell, ,,

Mr. Burrell, Broome Park.

The Rev. H. B. Carr, Whickham Rectory.

Dr. Charlton, Newcastle-on-Tyne.

Mr. Collingwood, Lilburn Tower.

Mr. Cookson, Meldon Park.

Miss Cookson, ,,

Mr. William Cookson, Eslington Park.

Mrs. William Cookson, ,,

Mr. Norman Cookson, ,,

Mrs. Arthur Coulson, Carham Vicarage.

Mr. Dickson, Alnwick.

Miss Eisdell, The Cottage, Cedars, Epsom.

The Rev. J. Elphinstone-Elliot, Whalton Rectory.

The Rev. T. Finch, Morpeth.

Dr. Fitzgerald, Folkestone.

Mrs. Foster, Selsey Rectory, Chichester. 2 copies.

Mr. W. Sidney Gibson, Tynemouth.

Mrs. Gore, 4, Cheriton Villas, Folkestone.

The Countess Grey, Howick. 2 copies.

The Rev. The Honourable F. R. Grey, Morpeth Rectory.

The Lady Elizabeth Grey, ,,

Colonel Somerset Grove, Mitford.   3 copies.

Mrs. Somerset Grove,   ,,   3 copies.

The   Rev.   H.   Teush-Hecker,   Misterton   Rectory,
Lutterworth.

Colonel Teush-Hecker, Folkestone.   3 copies.

Mrs. Teush-Hecker,   ,,   3 copies.

Miss F. Hepple, Mitford.

Mr. Hodgson-Hinde, Stella Hall.

The Rev. B. P. Hodgson, Hartburn Vicarage.

Mrs. Hodgson,   ,,

Mr. Robert Hodgson, Whitburn.   2 copies.

Mr. J. G. Hodgson, North Dene, Gateshead.

The Rev. Thomas Ilderton, Ilderton.

Lady James, Betshanger.   2 copies.

Mr. Edward James, Swarland Park.

Lt.-Colonel Johnson, The Deanery, Chester-le-Street.

The Lord Kenyon, 12, Portman Square.

The Lady Kenyon,   ,,

Miss Dawson Lambton, Swinburne Castle.

Mr. J. Langdale, Mitford.

Mr. Edward Lawson, Redesdale Cottage.

Mr. Thomas Marshall, Mitford.

Admiral Mitford, Mitford and Hunmanby.   3 copies.

Mrs. Mitford,   ,,   3 copies.

Mr. Townley Mitford, M.P., Pitshill.   2 copies.

The Honourable Mrs. Townley Mitford, Pitshill.

Major Mitford.   6 copies.

Mrs. J. P. Mitford.   6 copies.

Miss Emma Mitford.   2 copies.

Mr. B. E. Mitford, Royal Regiment.

Sir Arthur Monck, Bart., Belsay Castle.

The Duke of Northumberland, Alnwick Castle. 10 copies.

The Duchess of Northumberland,   ,,·   10 copies.

The Rev. E. C. Ogle, Kirkley.   3 copies.

Mrs. Ogle,   ,,   3 copies.

Miss Ogle,   ,,   3 copies.

The Rev. L. S. Orde, Shorestone Hall.

Mrs. L. S. Orde,   ,,

Mr. Orde, Nunnykirk.

Mrs. Orde,   ,,

Miss Pack, 32, Devonshire Place.   2 copies.

Mrs. Parker, Darrington Hall, Pontefract.

Mrs. Pidcock, 34, Imperial Square, Cheltenham.

Miss Potts, Mitford.

Mr. Pye, 4, Lancaster Gate, Hyde Park.   6 copies.

The Lord Ravensworth, Ravensworth Castle. 2 copies.

The Lord Redesdale, Batsford Park.

Sir M. W. Ridley, Bart., Blagdon.

Mr. Ridley, M.P.,   ,,

Miss Ridley,   ,,

Mrs. W. R. Sandbach, 10, Prince's Gate.

Mr. T. Eustace Smith, M.P., Gosforth House.

Mrs. Smith, Gosforth House.

The Rev. C. C. Snowden, Mitford Vicarage. 6 copies.

Mr. Harcourt Snowden, Thorpe Mandeville.

Mr. Shum-Storey, Arcot Hall.

Miss Shum-Storey,   ,,   2 copies.

Miss Nina Shum-Storey, ,,

Mr. Honywood Surtees, Benridge.

Mr. Swinburne, Whickam.

Mr. Goldie-Taubman, The Nunnery, Isle of Man.

The Rev. Charles Townley, Little Abington Vicarage. 3 copies.

Mrs. Gale Townley, Beaulieu, Newbridge, Bath.

Miss Walcott, 1, Victoria Grove, Folkestone.

The Rev. Canon Whitley, Bedlington Vicarage.

Mr. M. C. Woods, Holeyn Hall.

Miss Woods, Newcastle-on-Tyne. 2 copies.

Miss Yea, Monymusk, Aberdeen.

R. BARRETT & SONS, Printers, 13, Mark Lane, London.

www.ingramcontent.com/pod-product-compliance
Lightning Source LLC
Chambersburg PA
CBHW021801110726
47902CB00006B/1599